THE HUE: RED
PART 1

J.D. Roman

ISBN-13: 979-8-218-66197-7

Dedications

This book was created from the longstanding efforts of trial and error. There have been several incarnations of this book before it became tangible & for that I am grateful. This book takes from many influences: Anime, Psychology, Philosophy, American Politics & my military training. It was all coelesced when my car was involved in an accident & I was forced to focus & perfect this craft. For that, I thank God for granting me stillness.

This series is dedicated to my grandfather for all his help to ensure that both parts 1 & 2 get published.

To all the young Black adolescent males who are struggling to find your HUE, this book is dedicated to you. You all have inspired the bases for my main protagonist, Ashe. To all adolescents of all backgrounds at large, this book is also dedicated to you. To everyone who is struggling & reads this, keep searching for the HUE in you.

Acknowledgments

This series acknowledges all the efforts that my Psychology & Philosophy teachers have strived to instill in me. Haven taken several courses that trivialize existence & ethics, I wish to inspire that same level of discussion in this book series. This series further acknowledges all the great sergeants I have come aquainted with in the military. To my Drill Sergeants: Webber, Davis & Best, your commitment to me was well received. To my parents for continuing to support my efforts to succeed at my best potential, this acknowledgment is for you.

Table of Contents

Prologue

HISSS—goes the sound of the fire burning fiercely on the ground floor. It's a blaze with an abnormally proportioned flame that flails in one direction entirely without the winds directing it. With what seems like everyone in this section of town viewing this, a little girl grasped the ground and moves backward.

Her innocent face was in a nervous and frightened expression, while subtle sounds of breathing emits from her body. Dirt and dust in between her fingers, she cautiously moves far as she can from the fire. She eventually bumps backward into a townsperson who snatches her off the ground into an embrace.

"Are you ok, sweetheart?!" the woman asks the young girl. Her eyes were wide with her pupils constricted, allowing the girl to see the beautiful shade of her irises: VIOLET. The young girl tilted her head downward as if to conceal her face from the woman's. "Well, are you? Are you ok?" she asks again.

The little girl emphatically answers, "NO!"

"Granddad!" she calls out.

* * *

She stretches her arms from the lady's grasp. There, about six feet away from her, stood a man in front of the blistering blaze. It was a senile old man, who, for all intents and purposes, maintained a toned, healthy looking body for his age.

With outstretched hands toward the fire, he's hyperventilating. He emits a radiant, wispy substance. The substance formed around his hands before vanishing into the air in a smoky fashion. Increments of what seemed like microscopic diamonds were embedded in the red material before it dematerialized into the atmosphere.

His eyes widen as he stares paralyzed at the flame.

As the townspeople look closer with shock, there was a body laid in the fire burning in the smoke. Everyone looks at the man who stands before it and glares.

"You killed him!" one person shouts.

Others echo variations of the same phrase in the background.

The woman looks down in awe at the little girl. Unbeknownst to the girl, the woman was staring down at her until she looks back up at her violet eyes.

The lady looks at her innocent looking eyes and places the young girl back on the ground before backing up. She falls into the backdrop of people accusing the girl's grandfather of murder.

His ashy hands shake as he begins to understand what he's done.

"He tried to harm my granddaughter! You all saw it, right?" The man grabs his granddaughter hastily and pulls her behind him.

* * *

The crowd's mood turns to a menacing one and accusations of murder fill the scene. Everyone points toward the man who dramatically stands with his granddaughter behind him.

"STAY THE HELL BACK! ALL OF YOU!" he exclaims.

The Black HUE

The abundance of trees created the dark atmosphere, enclosing a ground made of a pitch black clay.

AND THERE I WAS.

"Is this a dream?" I struggle to say aloud.

It wasn't like anyone was around to hear me, or at least as far as I can see. I can tell this isn't my normalcy.

Typically, I can tell when I'm dreaming and this is not that feeling. This is not where I was seconds prior. But then again, WHERE WAS I? WHERE AM I? WHO AM I?

I know who I am. "Alabaster Ashe," I whisper to myself.

I raise off the earth.

Covered in the black terrain, my tucked in shirt had an emblem of a carnation on it with the words "Vanilla High" sewn in the flower's picture. Obviously, this is school clothing. More starts to come back to me. People call me by my last name, 'Ashe.'

I am sixteen years old and from Vanilla Stems, Alabama. I am . . . in 10th grade and.. I'm biracial or . . . BLACK. The White kids say I'm Black.

As a matter of fact, as I recall, I am the only Black person in town.

But what was I doing here?

Why am I laying in this dirt?

As I raise my head and look around, all I see is vast trees in an almost pitch-black forest. The sunlight crept through the top aerial view of these tall picturesque pines.

I reckoned I would've known better than to go roaming the forest of Vanilla Stems.

Especially when it's this dark.

I HATE THE DARKNESS.

From what I recall, I would say I am afraid of it. Dark surroundings, dark rooms, even black objects in motion. It all terrifies me! So how did I end up in this dark forest, covered in black clay?

The wind blows across my face and my afro rattles a bit. White as snow, it somehow evaded the black clay that covered my hands and clothes. My face was not so lucky, however. I wipe my eyes of the dirt so to make sense of where I was. It's not the best idea to wipe my dirty face with dirty hands, but my adrenaline is through the roof, and I feel sick to my stomach.

* * *

"Help! Somebody help me!" I screamed at the top of my lungs, spiraling in a circle. To no avail, I continue, "HELP. Help me." Off in the distance, I catch a quick glimpse of something I just knew couldn't be true.

It was a man in one of those tall pine trees that looked like half a football field away. I can barely make it out, but I am certain it is a tall man standing in a tree.

From afar, the shadowy figure was indistinct, leaving me questioning whether it was real or merely my imagination running wild.

I lean in with an eye squint and suddenly, *WHOOOSH*. A bird flies right past my peripheral and as it passes, the man in the tree disappeared. The bird lands on a limp branch and bounces on it.

"A crow," I mumble.

The bird triggers me and instinctively I breathe in a way that doesn't escalate my fear. I start to count backward from 7. I then exhale and open my eyes to a calmer me. This does, however, beg the question—where did I develop this technique?

I engage the scene once more and, to my horror, yet another crow shows up to a nearby branch.

It looked directly at my being, and I flinched.

It seemed, even from a distance, that I could make out the bird staring directly at me.

It stared directly into my eyes. I back away unnervingly and my hands sweat profusely, as does my face.

* * *

Trying to wipe my hand on my slacks, I feel something bulging from my pocket. It was a cubically shaped black box. I immediately stare at it with enlightenment. "Wait. Is it in here?" I pull out a diamond encrusted watch. It had a pure black center and shined in various colors when light touch the gemstones that meticulously adorned it. The time was exactly 7:00 am. The box that my watch came in had the words, "From mom" written on the inside as a memento.

I remembered. "I take this watch everywhere."

CRRRRAW—the crow caws. I look up and yet another crow pops into the scene. I look and count another and another. "8 . . . 9 . . . 12." I am soon surrounded.

Although I've never had asthma, I can imagine this feeling must be like an oncoming attack. All this darkness, all these black . . . creatures surrounding me. I can feel myself about to pass out. The birds' cries grew louder and more aggressive, forming an orchestra around me.

I can hardly keep up with my thoughts as I collapse to my knees. Hands clasped and above my head, I pray (another odd reflex I seem to have).

"God, please don't let me die in this forest. PLEASE GOD."

It was like you could hear a branch break in the silence.

The caws stopping as if to listen to my prayer. Immediately, without warning, all the birds descend on me.

They come in every direction. Impending doom was before my eyes. I sit, FROZEN . . . motionless to this attack. Suddenly, my chest burns. The feeling inside forms a sensation I couldn't recall feeling ever in my life. I feel my body about to spasm.

"What is this feeling? It's like I'm about to explode!" I catch a quick glimpse of the crows and it was almost like time slowed their descent down and they approached me in all directions in slow-motion. Not only that, the wind, the noise, the nearby ants heading into their hill all had SLOWED.

I rise to my feet and flail my arms out at the birds. Just then, I get a glimpse of a dial on a combination lock that spins clockwise to the number 5, counterclockwise to 60 and then clockwise to 5 again.

I scream. "NO!"

BOOM. The sound echoes through the forest, all through the trees and the nearby town. The crows stopped cawing, and the atmosphere was shrouded in black. Teary-eyed, I finally remember this moment from once before.

"This is exactly what I saw in a dream. I have been here before."

Above me is a black dome made of solid, yet semi-transparent black energy. The size of the dome far surpassed the height of the trees, and its width was astronomical.

A young girl, likely no taller than 5 feet, catches wind of this in her vista. Frail, pale and with two white ribbons on the opposing sides of her head, she leans in to grasp what she is seeing is real. Her youthful expression was more that of a curious young child than one who is interested in just the commotion of it all.

"Is that BLACK HUE?" she asks innocently.

* * *

Remarkably, her perspective isn't from the scene itself, but from a couple of miles away, observing the chaos from above.

She sits on top of a black stallion looking horse balloon, while wearing an all black dress. The balloon floats in midair within the distance of the black dome I was at the center of.

Her short and straight brown hair flows softly in the wind caused by the destruction I created. The ribbons on both sides of her head struggled to remain. "I hope no one is in the Arcane Forest, because that's forbidden," she says to herself. As she sits on the back of this floating balloon, tied to her waist, is a midsize brown carrying bag. It was filled with newspapers.

"Well, I mean, I should get back to work, but what do you think, Pegasus? Want to go check it out?" She looks to the balloon for answers. It does not speak nor has anything to suggest it be animate to speak.

A smile adorns her face. "OK! Let's go check it out!" The young girl then locks her hands around the giddy-up rope. Violet metallic energy poured from her hands. She gently compels the balloon to fly toward the dome.

In the middle of it all, I stare up at the completely dark dome made of this weird black energy. Under this dome, I tremble with both my wrists pointed upward.

Oddly, I feel the weight of the dome despite it being several miles above me. I can feel the weight of this black energy emitting above my hands and from my palms. It shrouds them and feels slightly heavy, but not unbearable. Another change I noticed was a cooling sensation. It came after the release of this darkness from inside me.

I try to process it all, but it was just too much. I slowly close my hands. It was slightly difficult, but I managed to ball my fists. Instantly, all the dome decimates. The metallic black colored energy fades away into the atmosphere and within thirty seconds, is no longer visible.

I look down at my hands in shock. My eyes widen to the narrowest constrict and all I can do is stare at my palms. They are unscathed and unblemished in the least. I notice my watch had fallen to the dark earth.

"My watch!"

I place it back in the container and back into my pocket. I look into the atmosphere and a cool breeze captured my face.

The entire wooded area—DESTROYED. There were no crows, no animals and there were no trees surrounding me for a lengthy distance. It was simply a field with black dirt and me, a kid from Alabama, lost in the woods.

"This feels too real to be a dream. Where the hell am I?!"

My hands smash into my head. I reflexively pull them down into a clasp.

I bow my head, saying, "Lord, forgive me for cursing."

"THE.. Lord?" a voice says from afar. I turned and found nothing on any side.

"The BLACKK . . . KEYY." I hear the voice whisper all around me. The voice drew out the words, so much so that I thought for a moment it had echoed. This was that same voice.

"Who is there? If you show yourself, I will . . . I will fight you. You better come in peace," I say nervously. The entire time, I'm about to soil myself. I try not to let it show on my face. Looking around, there was no one. I turned left. I turned right, and I even do a 180 and still nothing.

I stand still at the sight of a familiar image. A very tall man was standing in my distance. He stood still with a ripped jean and sweater ensemble. It looked as though standing before me was a corpse. Even from my distance, I can see this guy's skin was grey and dawned on his face, appeared to be a smile. I nervously think to move backward, but hesitate to do anything. It takes one step forward.

"THEE BLACKK KEYY . . ." It repeats this same phrase, again.

It immediately takes off, running in my direction. Pausing before I react, I then turnaround to run. I turn to notice this radiant energy emitting from its hands. It was in the color of violet.

"UNLOCK!" it says loud and resoundingly.

A mini-spiral of wind forms around me and spins my body around five times in a circle until throwing me onto my back.

I raise off the ground with a grimace and to my horror, it stood above me. Its eyes were black as the soil. It tries to swing its arm to grab me, but I jumped just in time.

When I jumped, it was no regular jump. I unbelievably jumped 12 feet high, my knees tucked to my chest. "Have I always been able to do this?" I ask myself. The creature then follows suit and jumps after me, basically at the same length.

It swipes at my foot, but a tiny pale hand, seconds before he could reach me, saved me. She grabbed me by my right hand. She struggled to stay ascended on her horse balloon.

* * *

"Don't worry, I won't let that Deadlock get you," she says. The thing falls back onto the floor of the earth with its menacing smile intact. We continue to ascend into the air. Once we got well over the remaining trees in the forest, my fear of the whatever was chasing me subsided.

I am now scared of falling stories from the sky. "HEY! Do you think you could get me back on the ground?"

She simply giggles. "Of course, silly, but if I put you back in the woods, those Deadlocks will get you. That's why this forest is off limits. YOU KNOW THAT!" She laughs with a carefree tone, as though my body isn't dangling from this high altitude.

My hanging position causes the balloon to tilt. "Here, grab this." She directs my hand to the saddle of the balloon and I get a good grip to pull myself up with both hands.

Now I am sitting on this small balloon, with limited space, behind this little girl.

I am lost for words.

"Are you ok? You look scared?" she asks innocently. I look at her and then at the ground. It was like looking at the ground from a plane about to land.

I felt like if I extended my arm I could catch a goose flying by. "Nothing is making sense in this nightmare. Please drop me back off at home or in a park somewhere? I don't care."

* * *

The young girl laughs at me as though I was jousting.

"You are cute! What is your name?" she asks.

"Alabaster Ashe. I live in Vanilla Stems, Alabama. I don't remember seeing you around town."

She looks at me and appears bewildered.

"Alabama? Isn't that an old territory of sort? I remember hearing about it in history class," she responds.

I look shocked. "ARE . . . we not . . . in Alabama?" I thought to check for the time, but at this altitude I decided not to risk dropping my watch. So I leave it in my pocket.

"Wait, what year is it? Isn't it 2023?" I ask.

She readily responds, "NO way." She reaches into the brown bag tied to her waist. "Here you are," she says, handing over a newspaper with the title, "Will the Warlocks Finally Bring Peace to Aether?" The date on the issued paper was: RED 1st, 4003.

I have a long-winded gasp. "4003? Ma'am, where am I?"

She turns to look at me. "This is Aether, silly. We are in the town of Medley. Don't you see it over there?" She points to various homes and people standing around dressed in modern clothing, but an odd scenery. I didn't see any skyscrapers or any cars. It just looked like regular people walking around with various agendas.

Something I noticed startlingly, is there were various races of people walking around with one another and besides each other. I saw dark-skinned people with light-skinned people, Asian looking people with Native American looking people and so on. I frequently observed olive-skinned, mixed-race children who looked like me, cared for by adults of diverse backgrounds.

It was baffling, and I can't help but to stare. "What is this place?"

"It's Medley, silly! Look over there. That's Grandlock Albedo's palace." She points to a gargantuan castle on the top of a nearby mountain and something about it gave me chills. It certainly looked like a palace with its unblemished black marble and its gates made of some kind of silver diamond. I could see it was being guarded fiercely, like the President stayed in it.

"If this isn't Alabama, are we even in the USA anymore?" I ask her.

She giggles again. "OH, this guy is confused! That black HUE has got him skipping backwards in time."

"Black 'HUE?'" I question. She turns to me with a smile.

"Yeah, you are a Blacksmith like me, but the Key you have is the rarest on the planet."

"What Key? What does all this mean? I don't know anything about some black HUE."

I almost forgot we had been floating midair on a balloon for the past several minutes.

"Well, I'm only thirteen, so I think you would be better off getting explained to by a professional. I was on my route when I saw all that black HUE you created and it caught my attention. Initially, I believed you to be Grandlock

Albedo. However, you're a Blacksmith with silvery white hair."

"Blacksmith?"

She turns back to the town.

"No one would believe there's a Black Locksmith with an active Black Key! With all that we go through, you must have appeared to save us. I am gonna call you 'Savior!'" she says.

I looked perplexed. On one hand, I like a name that's akin to Jesus, MY SAVIOR, but also I am confused on these terms: what is a "Blacksmith?" What is a "Grandlock?"

"OK, hold on Blacksmith, we are heading toward town," she says. Violet energy shrouds her hands and she takes off with me sitting behind her. I honestly had no time to grab her, but managed to not fall off.

She speeds through the sky and hovers above the town. There was oddly no pollution and this was the cleanest town I have ever witnessed. Then again, I don't recall leaving Vanilla Stems that often.

The feet of the balloon hover over a stream running through the town as she lowers it from midair to slightly above the water.

"If this is a dream, I have to admit, I am enjoying it," I say. She looks slightly bewildered. She turns her expression into a smile.

"Well, I am glad you are enjoying it, Savior."

* * *

"I go by Ashe, my last name," I respond.

She quickly retorts, "Savior Ashe! I think that has a ring to it!" She flies us back into the air for a moment until she sees something that catches her eye.

"There," she says. She flips the giddy-up rope on the balloon, which causes it to descend.

We finally reach the surface and I touch the ground for the first time in a while. In fact, because of my height no doubt, my feet touched the ground while the balloon still levitates above the surface.

The little girl in front of me, her feet are still dangling midair. We both hop off the balloon and she places the bag filled with newspapers back on top of it. "Ok Pegasus, go up, up and away!" She says this command with her two fingers thrusted into the air. They both have that violet foggy mist around them. The balloon goes back into the air, out of sight.

She walks past me down a short path that leads to this home. "Follow me, Black Keysmith," she instructs. I follow her, cautiously.

We pass a mailbox with the name "Pollux" written on it. We make it to the door and she knocks gently. I look around and it's rather quaint. Butterfly ornaments and a well kept flowering bed were just some of the decor.

It still felt like winter outside, however, but that didn't stop the plants in the garden from blooming. I glimpse at the little girl out the corner of my eye and immediately turned to her. It was only then that I noticed her eyes had such black irises. I almost mistook them for her pupils.

"Hey excuse me, I almost forgot, but what is your name?"

* * *

She turns to me, cheerfully. "Phoebe Saturn. I am the south side's papergirl."

"Nice to meet you, Phoebe. If you don't mind me asking, whose house is this?"

"This is none other than the History guru herself, Madam Celeste. I figured she'd be able to tell you about what happened to 'Alabama,' since she used to teach the neighborhood Blacksmiths history. She retired and runs a House where she teaches anthropology too."

Pausing briefly, I reply, "Anthropology? That sounds neat."

"Sure wish the people in town had your optimism, Savior Ashe. They don't say it out loud, of course, but it's commonly understood that people look down on those that focus on the past."

She turns to me with the biggest smile. "They say it's not *balanced*."

I pondered the emphasis she placed on the last word, "balanced."

"One more question Phoebe, I don't think I have ever seen someone with almost pitch black eyes. Is there a reason yours are? That . . . thing that chased me in the forest had eyes of that color, too."

"You are so cute! It's because I'm Black, silly, JUST LIKE YOU."

I turn to look at my reflection in the tiny glass on the door. In shock, I stare at my black eyes. My irises being the same color as Phoebe's and that demonic looking thing from the woods. It was then that it came back to me.

I was taunted as a child for being the only Black kid with these strangely colored eyes. It randomly comes back to me.

* * *

The door opens and I snap out of my daydream. An elderly woman, matching my skin tone and Phoebe's height, answered the door.

She and I lock eyes for a short period.

I have this odd inner feeling that I wonder if she shared.

"Hello, Madam Celeste! You'll never guess what I found. This is Alabaster Ashe, and he has an ACTIVE BLACK KEY!"

The old lady stares back at me and I couldn't get a "hello" so much out of her, let alone out of my own mouth. "You . . . you have returned," she says.

Hueman

I stand there frozen in front of a woman I've never met, but oddly feel connected to. Now here she stands, suggesting that she recognizes me. "Madam Celeste, you know this young male?" Phoebe asks with the widest eyes.

"I cannot say I do, but I've had dreams of a boy just like this when I was a kid. A boy with white hair being held in the hands of a man with hundreds of onlookers and then, POOF, he disappeared. I would have this memory for years and years, nightly. THEN, I just stop having dreams," she responds. Celeste was looking me up and down the entire time she recalled this dream.

Oddly, it triggered a memory of my own. I was a young boy looking up at my father and he tells me, "YOU'RE ADOPTED." Young me looked up with tears too heavy to carry. I zone back into the present day after having this memory. "I'm adopted!" The two look at me with confusion written in their expressions.

"I just remembered, I'm adopted. Where is this place? What is going on? Is this like a virtual reality or some sort?" I fire off question after question, to no avail.

* * *

Phoebe looks into Celeste's eyes with excitement. "Madam Celeste, look! This boy has an active Black Key."

"You did say that, didn't you, Phoebe?" Celeste inquires, while looking closer in my direction. Her eyes too, were jet black. She halts and looks as though she saw danger. I look around as though something not in my viewpoint was amiss.

"Wait right here, sweetheart." She goes back inside and closes the door in our faces. Phoebe and I just stopped and stared at one another.

A minute or so after, she reopens the door. In her hand she held a small bracelet with a black core holding together various tiny triangles. The white triangles were sandwiched together around the black band. "Here, place this on, sir," she requests and places the bracelet on my wrist. It fastens automatically once it touched my skin and I immediately feel something in my body change.

It fastened at a tiny rectangular jewel at its center that was clear until it touched my wrist. It immediately turned black, like a mood ring. I stare in slight awe.

"OH, you went to get a 'keychain.' Definitely shouldn't be outside without one of those, Savior Ashe!" Phoebe's words make me examine what this "keychain" even was. Closer examination I can see that the triangles, while attached to the black core of the bracelet, actually can spin around in tiny slits, which is why I can feel the core without the tiny shapes irritating my skin.

The jewel was the most eye catching, however, I wondered what the purpose of this was. Instantly, one triangle spins around rapidly. It changes colors to black and stands out amongst the several white triangles. "Now, why did that happen?" I ask curiously.

* * *

"Well, it would seem, young lad, that Phoebe was not telling a lie," Celeste says, her eyes widened. "You truly do possess an active Black Key and it looks like you have unlocked your very first combination." Celeste ends the sentence jovially.

"You look confused. Let me explain. This is a keychain. It prevents your HUE from destructive combinations that can kill someone or vastly change the environment," she says.

I think to myself how I could've used this about 30 minutes ago. "Now, if you look at the triangle that changed colors, it'll show you that combination." I listen to Celeste and immediately take a look at the triangle. Though small, my eyes discern the numbers "5" followed by "60" and "5" all in separate corners of the triangle.

"5, 60 & 5. That doesn't sound like a lucky lotto combination," I joke.

"Every combination will be in threes," Phoebe states.

"My goodness, someone like you must've been so scared when your Key revealed itself. Phoebe, do you know if he possesses any other Keys other than this?"

"I do not, Madam Celeste. But I think just having the Black Key alone makes him so special! The great HUE that surrounds us must've sent him here to fight for the plight of the Blacksmiths."

"What exactly is this 'Black Key' you all keep mentioning?" I ask in an irritated tone. I can feel myself slowly becoming angry with all this confusion and lack of answers.

* * *

"It . . . is just the most powerful Key in the world. For you to possess an active copy of it, this makes you one of only two Huemans that can make such a claim. The other being Grandlock Albedo." Celeste pauses briefly. Her tone grew much more serious when speaking on my "Key."

The door opens wider and a young teenage girl pops her head out. "Hey Madam Celeste, is everything ok out here?" the girl asks. I almost collapsed before the girl could even ask a question. I was so stricken by her beauty, I just froze in place. I believed her to be White, or perhaps Middle Eastern in looks. Olive toned skin with perfect symmetry to her face, she had the most perfect pink lips. She had long, flowing brown hair and it was shiny with a wavy texture.

BUT what stands out the most are her golden irises that sat beneath the longest set of eyelashes. She was wearing no makeup and skin was flawless. We make eye contact and I immediately felt a connection. It was one that made me sick to my stomach. Looking at her, I can tell she felt something, too.

"Ashe, are you ok?" Phoebe asks. I feel my stomach growing heavy until I fall to the ground and pass out. The three ladies all stare in disbelief while I lay to the ground.

Snow starts falling slowly from the atmosphere.

I think I'm dreaming. This was a familiar setting I had remembered from childhood. Surrounded in darkness, there I stood in a vast but vacant area of pitch black. I start to tremble before I begin to practice my breathing technique to calm myself. Looking around, my eyes are drawned to an outline of a closed door in the far distance.

* * *

I can hear something calling my name from behind it. "Ashe . . ."

Though a whisper, it echoed around the darkness. "Asheee . . ." The closer I got to the door, the louder it got. "ASHEE . . ."

I get close enough to see a chain on the door with a padlock, and immediately I hear a loud knock from the other side of the door. *KNOCK*

Startled, I awaken in a pool of sweat. Shaken and nervous, my eyes darted around, frantically scanning my surroundings. I could tell I was lying on a couch indoors. I see out the corner of my eye that there are various artifacts on shelves and a fossil on the wall entitled "The first Hueman skull." Surely, "Hueman" was a typo.

There was a television under the skull with what appears to be the news. A woman with purplish eyes is on the screen talking about the weather. "There's going to be a tornado stepping down in Medley. It is approaching at any second, so we have the Disaster Locks here to dispel it." The screen shifts to three individual men all dressed in black jackets with their hands out and pointed forward. All three were of different races and skin tones: one Black, one White and another I assume is mixed with both.

One thing they all shared, like the woman, they all possessed a different shade of purple-colored eyes. I look perplexed as I see the eye of the tornado approaching in the near distance. "Okay, you guys ready?" one man asks, as the other two nod.

"UNLOCK!" they say in unison.

Violet-colored energy emits from their palms and surrounds their hands.

* * *

The tornado shakes and turns until it eventually disperses. The violet energy dissipates and the three men high five one another. I look on amazed and the screen switches now to another young lady. This time tannish skin to the point I could not identify her race and her eyes were a bright colored yellow.

"Now, in a developing story, authorities are still trying to make sense of the cataclysmic disaster that took place in the Arcane Forest," she says, causing me to gasp.

They were showing the scene of the debris I left when my body created that black dome. "Authorities sent crews to further clean up the carnage of dead crows and small tree-dwelling animals.

"In an odd turn of events, authorities say they reached out to Grandlock Albedo and his administration has responded with 'No comment,'" the lady on the screen further detailed.

The more I watch, the more I felt a slight pinch on my lower legs. I think they are going numb, but I don't know why. Further inspection finds that a young boy, who couldn't be any older than Phoebe or taller for that matter, was sitting criss-cross on my knees.

I would've immediately classified him as Mexican, with his dark olive skin and eye shape, but his reddish-brown hair and freckles made it slightly difficult to pinpoint his ethnic group. His eyes were a dark brown, the most normal I had seen all morning. "I know it's rude, but I just don't know if I should trust you yet, sir," he says.

"I'm the only man in this house, so I have to protect the ladies at all costs. Just by the looks of you, I don't know any young Black Locks with white hair. So obviously you're not from here. If you're a ne'er-do-well, fair warning, I will defend Madam Celeste's home to the death," he says this in an emphatic tone.

* * *

"I am not a ne'er-do-well," I say sincerely. The little boy's entire expression changes to a smile.

"Ok, good to know, sir," he says.

I respond nervously, "No problem, little guy. Do you think, um, you could raise off my knees a bit?"

"OH, right!" he responds. He hastily raises off me and stands on the floor. Small statured, he sports a long brown sleeve and modern jeans with socks that had the roman number "II" written largely on both pairs.

I notice something familiar in his pocket. "Hey, is that my watch? Give it back to me! That's important." I jump to my feet, reaching toward the little boy.

"Wait, wait, please let me fix it. LOOK." He shows me the watch and to my horror, some of the diamonds are chipped off. "See, you took a nasty fall outside and messed the watch up. Let me fix it for you," he says.

With the watch in one hand and his other hand on top, that same energy from before starts to emit from his palms. This time it was a metallic brown. "Craft, unlock!" he says, and once he raised his hand off it, my watch was back to looking brand new.

"Here you go, sir. Madam Celeste, your visitor woke up!" He called her and I can hear her making her way into the room from some area in the house.

I look around and really try to gauge where I was. "Am I still asleep? No, I just woke up from a dream."

The boy looks at me innocently and asks, "Do you always talk to yourself?"

Of course the answer is yes, but I wasn't going to freak the kid out.

I locate the box I had my watch in on the shelf next to the wall and approach to grab it. I notice it smells like cooking in the home, so I'm guessing the old woman was in the kitchen making something for dinner.

I looked at the clock on the wall and it most certainly was about 7 pm, so it only made sense, I guess. I must have been unconscious since this morning, after . . . that thing I conjured. That's kind of weird. I don't recall ever sleeping that long before.

Nothing was making sense. I see a calendar on the wall and the title of the month was "RED" and there was a circle on the "1st." It also has "Year 4003" in the top left corner. "Phoebe wasn't lying. I'm in the future. But how?"

Someone walks into the room and to my surprise it was not Madam Celeste, but that girl. She walked in, causing my stomach to feel empty once more and immediately turns the channel from the news. "Jasper, why must you watch the news? It's so depressing," she says, turning to me with a soft smile. I barely can maintain eye contact. If my skin could blush, I'd be the reddest shade of shyness.

"I just want to know what's going on in the world, Eve. Is that so bad?" he cries. She walks over to me and places her hand on my shoulder.

"Madam Celeste will be here in a second. 'Ashe' was it?" I immediately feel my toes curling at the sight of a girl touching me, let alone someone as beautiful as her. "That's a very interesting name. Is that like a play on the term 'ashes?' Madam Celeste said you had an active Black Key, but do you possess the Red Key of Fire as well?" she asks.

Baffled, I respond, "What exactly is the 'Key of Fire?' I have never heard of it?" Her and the young male's faces look more confused than mine.

"Maybe he lost his memory when he fell. It'll come back to him," says the boy.

"I think he's just delirious from waking up," she responds. She points her index finger and her middle finger upward and all others downward with her right hand. "Unlock!" she says. Immediately, metallic gold energy swirls from her palm to the top of her fingers to form a spiraling ball of light above them.

She approaches me and places the ball of light toward my face. "Don't be scared, Ashe. Just talk into the light," she tells me. I notice her wrist has the same bracelet I had on earlier, but the jewel on hers is gold (the same color as that misty spiritual energy from her palm).

"Tell me, from your recollection, what is your name and where are you from?" she asks.

With the light spiraling next to my mouth, I nervously answer, "My name is Alabaster Ashe. I am from Vanilla Stems, Alabama."

She looks in shock before continuing, "One last thing, Ashe, what year were you living in Alabama?"

"Last I checked, I was living in 2023," I state, and her expression was as though she saw a ghost. Jasper looks and too begins to dawn the same expression. "Is there something wrong?" I ask.

Celeste finally enters the room. She snatches off her huge bifocals and places an enormous book on a nearby table in the room. "I am sorry to keep you all waiting but I finally found the state of Alabama and guess what? According to this book, we are geographically exactly where that would be, almost 2000 years your future, Mr. Ashe."

Celeste's words ring in my ears, but I feel unsurprised. I clearly am not in Alabama anymore. The real question is, IS THIS ALL A DREAM? I turn to the girl and the ball of light disperses into the gold energy before disappearing.

She takes a deep breath before calming herself. She looks at me with a tiny smile. "Where are my manners? I never formally introduced myself to you. My name is Evening Dawn Gold. You can call me 'Eve.' I just used the Detective combination to see if you were being truthful.

"Had you lied, the light would've dispersed as it did a lot earlier, BUT IT DIDN'T. I believe you, 100%. You truly are from Alabama." She says this all softly, but I sense an unease with her. It was as though she was still a bit hesitant about accepting me.

"Here's the question though: what exactly made you come here now from your time period?" the young boy asks.

"I am just as confused as you all. I am still struggling to accept any of this to be real," I respond.

"OH, it's real and so is your active Key," Celeste says with a charitable grin. Something is not right about all this. Did I fall into a time loop? Did I time-skip? In between me contemplating an answer, Celeste points to the black box that's exposed in my pocket.

It grasped her curiosity as she approach to grab it. I hesitated at first, but allow her to hold it the second time she reaches for it. She pops the box open and, to her amazement, my watch was shimmering in all its diamonds gloriously. Her mouth drops and I question her intent. She takes another look at my clothes and touches the flower design on my shirt. "Alabama?"

Celeste has the entire room looking at her attentively.

Eve turns to me with a soft smile. "You look very confused. It's okay, I'll explain."

Celeste looks at my wrist and immediately goes on alert. "HALT. Give him that keychain first." The young boy walks up boldly and places a bracelet with the triangles on my wrist.

The clear jewel immediately saturates with color until completely metallic black. Looking in it, it resembles a glittery cosmos. One triangle changes black, with the same numbers as before: 5, 60 & 5. "I am sorry I didn't introduce myself earlier. My name is JASPER BISTRE," he cheerfully says. I nod nervously and then look around, as something felt odd.

"Hey, where is Phoebe?"

"Oh, she had to go finish her paper route. She is a hardworking Blacksmith. She's so impactful on this side of town and doesn't even realize it," Eve says.

"Eve, he doesn't know what a 'Blacksmith' is. Locks didn't exist in his time. Educate him," Celeste sternly instructs her, and Eve agrees.

"I heard Phoebe use the term on the ride here. I am still uncertain what makes someone classified as 'Blacksmith.' Is it like calling someone 'Black' in my day? I hear you're an anthropology teacher, Madam Celeste. I assume you know about my time's different racial categories." Celeste takes a moment to look up into the ceiling.

From her expression, I could tell she was trying to recall or think heavily about something.

"My adoptive White dad raised me as Mixed-Race, but everyone in town called me the 'Black kid.' As far as I know, at least one of my biological parents is Black," I say. I felt the need to give more context for my answers.

Jasper takes an interest. "Did all mixed-race people from your era have white hair as teenagers? Like, is that the norm from your time period, Mr. Alabaster?" I take a moment to steer away from my serious face and laugh a little.

"No Jasper, in fact, my hair color is just as odd as my eye color from where I come from. It's like I got the White side in my hair, the Black side in my eyes and my skin just is in between," I say jovially.

"Balanced," Eve says in a generous tone. But the term feels like it carries more weight than I may interpret it. Celeste points to the sofa and looks in my direction. After staring back in a shy manner, I stroll to the sofa and take a seat. Jasper follows and sits next to me. He made sure to measure a safe distance before sitting next to me.

"Just wanted to make sure to give you a comfortable amount of space. I sense a little leeriness about me since you woke up and saw the watch in my hand. For that, I apologize."

I was struck by how articulate he was. But when he spoke, I could tell there was a sincerity about him. "I appreciate that, man. I reckon I should thank you for fixing my watch," I say to him.

He laughs. "What's a 'reckon?'"

Celeste takes a sigh before turning to Eve. She suspiciously was not commanded to sit with Jasper and myself, nor did she make an effort.

"We are going to need a light show, ma'am," Celeste says.

Eve retorts back to her in a peaceful and refined tone, "I figured. You do all the talking and let me handle the rest, Madam."

Celeste picks up an artifact as she talks. "The eye—the Hueman eye. If you look into the iris, it mirrors the soul." The artifact was in fact a large clay crafted eye with a large black pupil and surrounded by a peach colored iris.

"Long gone are the times that sentient beings judge one another by superficial skin tones," Celeste says. "Instead, we go off the eye." She places the eye back on a shelf. "Ready, Eve?" Celeste asks. She nods and positions her hand in the air.

"Craft, unlock!" Eve spouts and the metallic gold energy floods her palms right before forming a spiraling globe midair. The landmass on the globe looked familiar, but I have to ponder on it before I identify it.

"Pangaea! I remember it from school!" I say.

"Oh no, my dear," Celeste starts up, "this is not pre-human Pangaea. This is post-human Aether. As in the supercontinent of today."

'Aether' sounds like something out of sci-fi or some kind of alkaline metal. I tune out my thoughts so I can pay close attention to Celeste dropping knowledge and Eve's light show.

"It was 2023. The astronomers of the best space shuttle exhibit in the world foresaw a tragedy miles away heading toward Earth."

* * *

As she speaks, Eve uses the light to change images to depict Celeste's every word. "A meteor the size of the moon flailed toward the planet. Its size was compromising, and the astronomers immediately knew they could do nothing to stop its impact. Instead, after informing the humans they only had 49 hours to live, they immediately fell to their knees asking for mercy and worshipping their respective deity, or shall I say, many of them did this. The majority went outside in anticipation.

"The moment those humans understood they would perish together, all wars stopped. The jailing system stopped. Cops killing the innocent stopped. The stock market stopped. It was the most peaceful 49 hours since humans became a species. In humanity's final hours, people all across the world held hands.

"From your day's America to Asia. This was the longest handheld chain ever conceived. It was said to loop around the globe 3 times altogether. All stood in solidarity for the apocalypse." Eve shows the meteor coming into the Earth, but instead of destroying it, the meteor disperses into millions of pieces.

"To their surprise, the moment the meteor hit the Earth's atmosphere, it disintegrated. The meteor shattered into trillions of tinier pieces. This completely covered the Earth and there was not a section of the world that had not any debris from the meteor," Celeste says.

The light show showcases the debris falling into 1,000s of straight lines downward. "The Arcane Forest, that's not too far from town, was the site that caught the most impact of the meteor," Celeste states. That made sense. I guess that pitch-black coloring on the ground was from the meteor's remains.

That means that the meteor was rather potent.

Madam Celeste continues, "The black meteor's ashes blanketed everywhere, leaving only remnants of a great catastrophe that united the world. It went from a danger that had everyone thinking they were about to perish, to a reflection on human values. This made worldwide press and everyone began to wonder what the substance was that created the meteor. It did not match any known elements on the periodic table.

"In fact, those who were outside holding hands received a small dose of it, as it blanketed the world. This grew the concern over studying and understanding its effects on the humankind."

Eve creates an image of a pair of DNA strands. It was intriguing to see, but I questioned the reasoning. I was fully invested in where the story was about to go now. Celeste says, "Scientists start studying people who, 90% plus, were standing outside and had a front row interaction with the meteor. What they found was that everyone they brought into their laboratories had alterations in their DNA.

"As Eve is displaying here, there was a new chromosome with a new set of genes added to the people of Earth. The 47th chromosome came as a shock to the scientific community that deemed it to be a scientific anomaly. That is, of course, until more and more people came into the labs and tested positive for this extra chromosome. Along with the presence of a new DNA blueprint, this new version of mankind exhibited odd abilities. They were able to leap into the air freely as far into trees and on top of houses in some cases.

"Their bodies withstood varying temperatures better. Fire still burned, but seldom left anything beyond a tiny irritation on the skin that healed within a day or two. WE ran quicker and for longer periods of time. Stamina and endurance differed greatly from your day humans. Most notably, however, was the unfamiliar presence of the *Keys*."

Celeste takes a quick break from speaking, and all eyes turn completely to Eve's light show. Seven orbs form in a circle. Each with a distinct color and spiraling in synch. There was: red, brown, gold, green, blue, violet & black, respectfully.

"When scientists became aware that every person now had a blueprint in their DNA allowing them to control some facet of nature, this became the nucleus of naming them 'KEYS,'" Eve says.

"Why 'Keys?'" I question.

"Humanity had always pondered through science and philosophy how to tame the world," Celeste responds. "So the Key is the answer. It is the answer to mankind's plight since the birth of the species," she says. "It is also something to be said that when that meteor crashed down on us, it changed us. Now everyone has a Key or some variation of Keys. This is because of the meteor linked our souls to the environment."

Celeste then points to the orbs and in order goes down the list: "The Red Key: the Key of Fire; controls fire, temperatures and conflagrations. The Brown Key: Key of Earth; controls dirt, sand, ground, and minerals. The Gold Key: Key of Lightening—" she pauses to me, interrupting,

"Lightning?" I ask.

"NO—Lightening, it, however, does control light and electricity. It is Eve's signature Key," she says and Eve smiles at the recognition. "The Green Key: Key of Wood; controls plants, shrubs, germinates, mosses, and many non-sentient entities that grow, such as bacteria. The Blue Key: Key of Water; controls water in all of its forms, from ice to rain to snow. The Violet Key: Key of Wind; controls air, turbulence and all the gases. Including the noble gases like helium. Lastly, the Black Key: the special Key that speaks fear into the hearts of many. Though common, over some time, it has lost all of its brilliance."

* * *

"Everyone who has it today, has remnants of a once great Key."

"What do you mean by remnants?" I ask Celeste with a confused expression.

"Vestigial. Everyone who has a Black Key inside them now has a vestigial Key, meaning there is no expression of it. It no longer works as it once did," she responds. "When it did work, the Black Key was said to control Time, Space & Dimensions. It is known colloquially as the Void Key."

Celeste's words pierce through me.

I try to take it all in, but I'm in awe at the potential this "Key," can bring. All I can do is stare at my palms with my mouth trembling. "I know it's a lot to ingest Ashe, but Celeste is giving the meat and potatoes of this time period. Once you understand these fundamental facts, everything else will fall into place," Eve reassures.

"Okay, so did I time travel here with this 'Void' Key?" Celeste pauses before answering me.

"I suppose so. It just feels like . . . I mean, you look so familiar. IT CAN'T BE." Celeste continued to ponder a response.

"Well Madam Celeste, you can rest assured if you do not know the answer to that, Grandlock Albedo will know," says Jasper.

I look toward Celeste in slight inquiry. I keep hearing this guy's name, yet no one has explained him to me. "YES! YES, Jasper, that is very true. Grandlock Albedo is omniscient. He definitely knows of your presence or hell, maybe even sent for you," Celeste says hurriedly.

* * *

"What makes him so special? And why is he called a 'Grandlock?'" I question with an expression of disbelief on my face.

"Well, firstly, a Warlock is an official that holds a high-ranking role in laws and decision making in any given town. Every town has seven Warlocks that run it. This is equivalent to your time's mayor or governor. What makes Albedo a standout amongst them is that 1.) he is the oldest Warlock in existence. People say Albedo is only a couple of generations younger than the first Huemans. 2.) Grandlock Albedo is 1 of several 1,000 births that result in a person being born with all seven Keys. Such individuals are called 'skeletons.' The community always cultivates skeletons to be the natural born leaders.

"Almost every town has a skeleton that leads them. Respectfully, their rarity means not every town has one. 3.) And the most important reason Albedo is the most beloved Warlock is because he is, or shall I say was . . . the only known Hueman with a functioning Black Key. His Key has been around longer than the vestigial status that overtook the Black Key. Therefore, his omniscience is understood, because his Key enables him to see present, future and past."

Celeste pauses briefly to gaze at me in my eyes. "With such importance as he, Albedo is not just a Warlock. Everyone in the world refers to him as 'Grandlock Albedo.' Grandlock Albedo is effectively the President of this new world you've found yourself in and Medley is the beacon," says Celeste.

I take a moment to process it all. Time, space & dimensions at the palm of my hands? This place just cannot be real. NOT the guy who was the hated "Black kid" growing up? NOT the guy whose last recollections are being made fun of for being Black with white hair as a teen? NOT the guy who is utterly afraid of the color black? This place has to be a dream!

* * *

A brief pause comes over me. It felt like a trance where I had a flashback in real time. A time when I was a child playing baseball with the neighborhood kids. The boys never wanted to pick me. I got picked occasionally and even at seven, they made me know I was the 'Black kid.'

"My mom says I'm not supposed to play with him," one kid said. He throws his mitten on the ground and walks away off the field.

"Good job 'Black Ashe!' Now we're down a player," says another disgruntled kid.

When it was my turn to bat, I would always approach it nervously, but when the ball came at me, it was as if time slowed down to the nanosecond so I could hit it relatively easily. It would go black around me sometimes and I would start shaking, but the ball would come in slow motion.

SMACK—it flails into the air. Someone ran to retrieve it in the backfield. He throws it at the guys in front who tried to tag me with it. But with an instant, *WHOOOSH*—I would jump straight over his head and land on the home base.

"How did he do that?" questions one kid.

"I think it's because he is Black," responds another.

"Definitely, that's why mom said to stay away from 'Black Ashe,' because he is using some type of black magic," yet another kid says.

"EXACTLY! Look at his eyes! Why are they so black?!" asks one of those awful kids.

I slowly come back to the present. In the present I catch a glimpse of my eyes in a mirror in the room. Black as the energy that emits from my palms. "I was able to jump over those kids' heads when I was in elementary school. That same darkness I saw in the forest is the same that I would have nightmares about all growing up." I say aloud and all in the room listen. "And my eyes . . . they've always been this odd color."

"Don't beat yourself up, Ashe. Here, many people have those eyes. What is a curse to some is a blessing to others. See, the eyes are the windows to our souls. As mentioned before, the meteor's dust forced an evolution in our species. It forced our souls to combine with the environment.

"So everyone you see has an eye color that shows their Key. The Keys are just our souls linked to the world around us. Those with dominant Fire Keys have variants of red-colored irises, while dominant Water Keys have variants of blue-colored irises, etc. What makes you special is that Black eyed people, or 'Blacksmiths,' 'Black Locksmiths,' etc. as we call anyone that possesses a dominant Black Key, they are expected to have a dominant vestigial Key. However, yours is not, and once you understand the hierarchy in this world, you'll soon see why this is a tremendous deal," says Celeste.

Eve ends her light show, and the gold energy slowly evaporates. "It's called HUE," she goes on, "When you use a combination, your HUE always pours into your palm and then when you say 'unlock,' you produce whatever combo you sought, as such. That's why we are called Huemans. The Key is the soul-link, and the HUE is its expression." Eve walks closer to me jubilantly and holds me by my hands.

"Alabaster Ashe, it is truly my pleasure to meet you and I think you're going to be the most important figure in this century," she says. I struggle to look her directly in her eyes.

I have known no one to admire my eyes the way she does. "It . . . it's my pleasure to meet you as well, Eve." My mind almost glitches, like something about her makes me feel so uneasy.

"Well, after dinner you ought get some rest in. Tomorrow is going to be a long day. We have to go see Albedo and pray he has something positive to say about you," says Celeste.

"What could be the negative?" I ask curiously.

"Well, his omniscient ability would mean he could know you were coming for some time. So I go so far as to say, he sent for you. But for a skeleton to seek another Lock with the Black Key, means something very important must be about to occur," Celeste ends.

What makes you balanced?

The clock ticked slowly above the window. Drearily, I look directly at the clock from my side of the room. It ticked slowly, but with no visible movement in its hands.

In fact, the general mood of the room was one where everything felt as though time had stopped. I felt paralyzed in this state and only my eyes could move. I lower them from the clock to the window and even the snow outside has frozen in time. Only the ticking clock was audible.

"Where am I?" I soon grew horror at the sight of a crow flying onto a tree limb. It, along with the limb, are the only things with motion that I could see. It stared sneeringly at me. I feel my insides trembling, but it was not displayed outward in my mute body. Suddenly, the bird jumps from the limb and crashes into the window, making a loud thud—*BAM.*

I awaken from this dream sweating. From the looks of it all, I was in a bed tucked in nicely. In front of me was a different window than was in my dream. Above it, a different clock. "Was it all a dream? Am I really home?" I question. I try to raise at a ninety-degree angle and immediately bump my head. My thoughts come to their senses and I realize I'm in a bunk bed.

* * *

Because I'm an only child, it couldn't have been my room. I roll over to the floor on all fours and waste no time rising to my feet. I go over to the window and open the curtains to reveal the true sunshine hidden behind them.

It was a bright and sunny morning with limited snow from the previous day.

I slowly turn to see people once again of different physical features walking in harmony up and down the streets. There were those with physical features like that of Asians, Whites, Blacks etc. walking in harmony and some holding hands as if to suggest they are dating.

I was the only minority I ever knew before. All these cultures, I only seen on television. Oddly, it felt refreshing. It brought on a warm sigh to me to not be the only minority in town.

I noticed they all would be more so walking in sync with those with similar eye colors. I noticed all the green-eyed people walking in groups laughing together and same with blues. Most groups that passed, however, had at least one black-eyed friend with them.

The boy I swore was Mexican with freckles walks into the room. "Awe, you're up. Come, Mr. Ashe. We have breakfast every morning at this time and Madam Celeste will be ready to disown us if we are late," he says.

"Ok . . . Jasper?" I had to question if I had remembered his name correctly, but it didn't even matter since he had already left out the room. I look over to see my school clothes folded to the side and recalled showering last night before borrowing clothes from Eve.

This explains why the pajamas felt tight and had flowering buds as decoration. I walk down the hall and catchup to the young boy. "Hey Jasper, do malls still exist? Depending on how long I'm here, I am going to have to get some new clothes."

Jasper looks at me sternly. "If your real worry is about clothes, then yes. There are venues to get new clothes. But, you'll need these." Jasper pulls out a thick coin. It was a little wider than a quarter and was jet black with a number "1" inscribed on it.

"In your time, there were so many currencies it was divisive. Nowadays, there's this universal currency." Jasper holds the coin as close to my face as his tiny arms would allow. "They are called meteor tokens. The same material as the meteor that hit Earth composes them."

"Well, what happened to gold and silver?"

"Can't use those if there are Locks like me who can control and conjure those substances. Currency means value, and what's more valuable than a substance no one can control?" he replies.

"I see your point."

We both head toward the kitchen. As we approach the kitchen, the smell of bacon overcomes the room. Toast pops out of a toaster and the aroma of southern style cooking fleshes my memory. I swear, something about this place I feel a personal connection to, but—I JUST KNOW NONE OF THIS CAN BE REAL. I look into the kitchen and the decor was so eclectic. It looked like ornaments from China, Africa, the Middle East and perhaps even India.

"Are these all objects you guys have found, Jasper?" I ask.

"Most, some bought. For a cheap price at that," he responds. However, I notice many of these ornaments have extremely good designs. Perhaps that meteor made some of them as well. Eve's flawless face caught my attention as she walked into the room.

I sense myself tightening up. Immediately, I couldn't make eye contact with her, though I wanted to so desperately. Her simple smile sent my head into a spiral as she made a plate for Jasper and me. She walks over to an empty seat and places a plate in front of it as well, then she makes herself one. She sits adjacent to Jasper and directly in front of me across the table.

I look down at bacon, grits and pancakes. "Madam Celeste should be in at any second, fellas. Ashe, I hope you fill up from the food. You have a long day today," she says. I put on an awkward smile before bowing my head to pray.

I clasp my hands, saying, "Lord, thank you for the food I am about to receive, for the nourishment of my body. In Christ we pray, amen."

I rise and open my eyes. To my surprise, both Jasper and Eve looked confused. "Who were you talking to, Ashe?" Jasper asks. It took me a second before I realized where I was.

"Oh, are you all not Christians anymore? I mean, is it not a thing in 4003?" I ask.

"NO. There is no Christianity at this time," Celeste says. "In fact, your concept of 'God' has changed." She walks into the kitchen and assumes her seat at the table.

The clock on the wall strikes 7 am. "Aww, right on time!" she says, looking toward Eve. "Thank you for cooking dear," she tells her. She then blows a soft kiss toward the teen girl.

* * *

"If no God, what do you all believe?" I ask sternly.

Celeste turns to me. "Good-morning to you too, Alabaster Ashe." I feel slightly embarrassed and my eyes look at the floor.

"Oh, my apologies, good-morning, Madam Celeste." Celeste then recollects herself and dawns a more inviting expression.

"Now, we have a more nuance view. 'GOD' may be the name, 'Allah,' etc. But we view the HUE as the prevailing force in this universe. It surrounds us. It dwells in us. Whatever IT is, It sent the meteor that changed us forever. It made us contractually bound to the natural world. It gave us the greatest answers to the problems that troubled humans. For that, you give respect to the HUE," she says.

That is a different take than I foresaw. I know that we Christians have this concept of a "Trinity" that involves Jesus dwelling in and working through us. So I guess that's . . . similar?

I nod at the knowledge with a fake grin. There is a reason I am here. If I just play along long enough, maybe I'll learn something from all of this and awaken with a VR headset on or something. This must be a trial of some sort.

"Oh, before I forget, Eve make for certain that you call to schedule Ashe and me a ride to Grandlock Albedo's lair," Celeste requests.

"Already done, Celeste. Ashe, your ride will be here in about 30 minutes, so make sure you're all well groomed, sir." Eve turns and looks at me with that response.

"Thanks." My eyes nervously look toward the ground. I can't bring myself to maintain eye contact with her for too long for some reason.

* * *

Jasper raises his hand for an inquiry. "Yes, Jasper?" asks Celeste.

"Grandlock Albedo should have sent someone to pick up Ashe, Madam Celeste. If he is omniscient, you shouldn't have to be burdened with spending tokens and booking flights for him," Jasper says in a serious tone. Celeste laughs.

"Oh Jasper, don't worry. We expect that knowing everything all the time would burden someone with many troubles in this world. We can do our part and pay a couple of tokens to go see him. No big deal!" Eve agrees with a nod and sips coffee from an ancient-looking mug.

"WELL, now that we are discussing today's main events, I would like to direct everyone's attention to the television screen," Eve says. She turns to the television that is across the kitchen, into the living room.

"Eve, you know I don't like a television playing while we eat," Celeste scolds.

"Madam, you will forgive me, but this is your special day." Eve winks at her and uses the remote to flip through the channels to what appears to be the news. The anchor, a mixed looking young girl, who interestingly looked about my age, was present on the screen.

"Today is the 2nd day of the start to a new year my fellow Aethereans, and what better way to ring it in, then by celebrating the life and accomplishments of Medley's very own, Madam Celeste? She is the first Blacksmith to grace the cover of 'Balanced' magazine. Her contributions to beauty changed the standard well over half a millennium ago on this very day. Since, she has dedicated herself as a 'Lockkeeper' in the community and continues to fight for civil rights for Blacksmiths all over Aether. For this, we wish you a wonderful day, Madam Celeste!"

* * *

The young reporter ends her speech, and Eve promptly turns the television off. I look in awe. "Over half a millennium? She's over 500 years old?" I whisper to myself, baffled.

"1006 to be exact, Ashe. Oh my, I had not realized it had been that long since I graced the cover."

Eve pulls out a well wrapped present with a bow on it. She hands it eagerly to Celeste, and she opens it. She was moved to tears by the surprise. "You made a mural of my cover. Oh thank you, Eve. I can't wait to hang it up." Celeste hugs Eve.

"Round of applause for Madam Celeste for still holding the crown as the most balanced woman," Jasper insists, and we all clap.

As I clap, I sense all eyes navigating to me. I felt odd clapping, as I did not know what this term "balance" meant in modern times. "Oh Ashe, you must be so confused. Let me explain," Eve says, turning to me.

"Balance is a philosophical principle developed around the same time as the first Hueman walked the Earth. It implies that we have more in common than different and establishes a more modern take on how we relate to one another. See, in your time, you all related to one another through skin colorations which led to superficial labels of social hierarchy. Nowadays, we relate by what you can do with your Key, which still causes divisions, but to a much lesser extent as you all's time pre-meteor."

Eve turns to the portrait of Madam Celeste in her younger days on the cover of a magazine. "We embrace a yin and yang styled principle all around the world. We also apply it to beauty standards. Olive or caramel skin tones are seen as more beautiful and balanced than extremely pale or dark skin. Eyes

47

too far apart or too close are not as beautiful as mid set eyes. The nose is more desirable when it is not too thin or round or too wide or pointy, as another example. Noses that don't point up or have a heavy hump are not as desirable as a plain straight downward nose. Supermodels of your time were widely thin, but somewhat curvy is seen as more desirable now. Hair that's not black or blonde, but brown is more balanced. Hair not too curly or straight, but wavy."

I come to realize the person she described is in this portrait of Celeste. The racially ambiguous look is apparently in fashion.

"We encourage people who don't fit the stereotypical balanced look to embrace what makes them balanced. That's why you will rarely see someone in this time period wearing fake hair, lots of makeup and it's socially frowned upon to wear those fake colored contact lenses of your time. But they still sell these items in small street vendors or alleys from time to time," Eve says.

"It's all about the inability to sway," Celeste says, looking at me.

"Stereotypical balance is all about looking right in the middle, which is symbolic of our times. So you, for example: have olive skin, a straight nose that does not sway too wide or thin. Oval face that's not too round or elongated and lips that are pleasantly balanced to not be too thin or wide. You do, however, have silvery white hair that sways too kinky, but that is what makes you, YOU! It's your balance sweetheart, so you should not be ashamed of it," she says.

I'm in awe. In this world, I'm kinda good-looking. Never could've been balanced back in my town. "You sway a little thin, but I see some muscles on you too," Celeste jokes.

Eve laughs, before she chimes in, "It's okay Ashe, I sway thin too." I get a good look at her body and am amazed at her proportions, though I turn quickly to not look like a creep.

"Yeah, I see."

She responds with a gasp, but a jovial one. "I didn't mean it like that, but I mean I don't see anything wrong with your proportions, Eve." I tried to clean it up, but it felt to no avail.

"You have a lot to learn about females, Ashe," Jasper says. An uproar of laughter ensues.

After I finished my breakfast, I immediately wash my plate in the sink and head back to the room I slept in. Changing out of Eve's pajamas and into my school uniform was something I looked forward to. I washed my face and brushed my teeth. I did a quick inspection of my white fro and thought it looked presentable.

Visibly, I looked like I was in deep reflection while walking back into the front room. I take a seat on the couch to wait. As cold as it was outside, I wish I would've brought a jacket.

Oddly, when I was in the woods, the temperature didn't feel too bad. I wonder if I always was this resilient to the cold? I remember being young and running in the snow with my arms and legs exposed. My father in the background thinking I was insane the entire time.

It was a random memory, but it was nice to start to rekindle some aspects of who I was before I opened my eyes in the forest. Maybe this'll help me retrace my steps and figure out how I got here. I don't know. This new world just seems . . . odd.

* * *

"Ashe?" Celeste inquires.

I turn to her tentatively. "You daydreaming again? The ride is almost here," she says.

I immediately stand up and walk with her toward the door. "Wait Ashe, take this," she says, pulling a coat out of the closet. It was a basic black coat. Thick and rather warm to the touch, it felt soft and well woven.

"That belonged to my husband before he passed hundreds of years ago."

I smile. It's an honor. I mean, her dead husband's coat kind of carries weight.

We walk outside into a more moderate temperature than expected. The snow had turned into frost, but the sun was slowly melting it all. Celeste takes a few steps and just takes a moment to soak in the radiant sunlight. The soft breeze seems to put a smile on her face.

"I love the natural world," she says. It seemed orgasmic to her.

"Are Eve and Jasper staying behind?" Celeste nods.

"Yes, dear boy. Eve will get started on dinner and Jasper has a test he is studying for."

I stop to think. A test?

"I haven't heard school mentioned once since I have been here. Are people, I mean 'Locks,' homeschooled in this time period?"

Celeste laughs. "No sweetheart, but I guess that's my fault for not explaining that sufficiently for you. So for starters, when you are young, everyone is taught formally by an instructor in the neighborhood. Some designated individuals take children of varied ages and educate them in the different areas of life that are important, with the permission of the town's Warlock. Math, Science, History, Language, Psychology and Philosophy are the core classes of focus. Followed by some form of self-defense course."

The last subject of her statement intrigues me. "Self-defense? So everyone knows how to fight?"

Celeste nods, "YES. But it's not just about fighting, but more so about becoming whole in your body and one with your own personal autonomy. Instructors teach every individual self-defense. We find this more useful than the guns of your time."

Celeste laughs and I smirk a bit, too. "Now getting back to what I was saying, here all students learn the core class curriculum and then at the onset of their Key, children then have the option to be homeschooled by their family members or leave home and join a special House to become a productive member of society. See Keys set in almost always around the age of 13. According to the World Constitution, once your Key presents itself, you may leave home to join a House that will teach you a specialty. All Houses are ran by Lockkeepers like me."

"What is a Lockkeeper?" I ask.

"Lockkeepers are designated instructors. We run Houses. I, for example, run a House teaching Archeology/Anthropology & Ancient civilizations. It is equivalent to your time's college.

"The moment your Key reveals itself to you, you may choose any House that you meet the requirements for. Most will attend their family's House to maintain heritage. Others, such that as Eve and Jasper, don't go the traditional route. Neither is better nor worse, but both are viable options."

Celeste's words make me think critically about how this could even work. The community trains you until your teens, then you're free to go—just like that?

"Hey Celeste, how do Warlocks know who is dangerous and, like maybe . . . has nefarious intentions with children?"

She sighs before responding to me. "Ashe, I don't know how best to break it to you, but crime is almost nonexistent in this time period. Sure, you get the occasional thief here and there, but this is a more balanced world. We have a universal currency that is more symbolic than practical. We have people who literally have a Key to grow food, so there is no world hunger. To top it off, Grandlock Albedo is omniscient. There are many safeguards against crime."

Celeste then laughs and taps me on the head playfully. I still am a little unsettled. Perhaps because I cannot fathom a world as structured as this, where everyone fits neatly into a role.

"Your world was riddled with wars and constant bickering, but we have taken a more balanced approach. Are you sick of me using that word yet?"

We both laugh, but it dawned on me that the ride to this Grandlock's lair was not here yet. "Wait, where's the ride Madam Celeste?"

She looks around. "I am not sure, Ashe. It should have already been here. This driver is almost always on time." Celeste looks up and points.

"Awe, there he is. Look up, sweet boy," she says. From the looks of it, there was an old school carriage attached to two horse balloons with lassoes. It glided through the air and finally lands before us in Celeste's yard.

* * *

The wind from the landing blows a tiny bit of snow on us both. "Now, let's hurry, Ashe!" We take a few steps and reach the door.

When opened, sitting inside the carriage was an elder gentleman of short stature. He had on a well-fitted suit and an elongated hat. A monocle was in his left eye, and his general expression was of displeasure. His skin was dark bronze and I could tell he had a white afro like mine, but it looked normal on him, given his aged face.

He was a very short man with violet-colored eyes. "Violet is the Key of Wind," I whisper to myself. I hesitate before getting into the vehicle. I slid into the middle and there was a seatbelt.

Looking up at him, I try to crack a smile to break the ice. He simply looked away with a grunt. Celeste gets in the carriage and closes the door. She fastens her seatbelt and relaxes. "Well, since when do you keep me waiting this long, Talon?" Celeste jokes.

He finally cracks a smile. "Well, rarely do I get a call to drop someone off at the Grandlock's gated residence," he responds in a similar joking manner. "Surely, Grandlock Albedo knows of your visit?" he asks. I look toward Celeste, slowly dropping my head down like a kid in trouble.

"Yes. He is all knowing, so he definitely knows," she responds. The driver nods and flicks the lassoes from the inside of the carriage. Through tiny holes, they traveled to the outside, where they were connected to each of the horse balloons.

"Unlock!" he calls. Violet HUE spews from his hands right before we lift off into the sky.

In less than 24 hours, I have been in the air more than I ever had back in my time. We soar at a moderate height above the town. Looking down, I get a great aerial view of what this town comprised. Parks, stores and outlets, but no skyscrapers. There were various homes made of differing material and different sizes. Two-story homes seem to be the norm. I saw nice looking gardens, but with no hoses attached to the houses.

Interestingly, though not shocking, there was not a car in sight. I didn't even see garages attached to these houses. Talon turns to me. "So young man, are you waiting for me to introduce myself first? It's customary around here to respect people's seniority and introduce yourself."

I gasp, "Oh my apologies, sir! My name is Alabaster Ashe. You can call me Ashe," I say hurriedly.

He pauses, "Ashe? That's a weird last name. Is it like short for 'asteroid' or? You know what.. NEVERMIND. You Blacksmiths have goofy last names."

For the first time since being here, I have felt offended about being a Blacksmith.

"Hey Talon, don't start that prejudiced talk. I have been very good to you all's business for 100s of years. Don't forget I know your great great-great-great grandmother who started this transportation business.

"She created this business because other Locks wouldn't take Blacksmiths from point A to point B, so I consider her a pivotal ally in civil rights. You bring shame to her."

Celeste's words echo as he seems to calm his mood.

"I'm sorry for being rude, Celeste. Earlier this week I saw a group of hoodlums fighting for tokens in an ally when I was dropping off a client at the

Doctor's office. They know that the world sees them a certain way and they do very little to change that perspective," he says with locked eyes on me.

"You are not a hoodlum are you, Alabaster?" he asks. I promptly shake my head "no."

He smiles, "Good. One of em even attacked the Mars guy's granddaughter yesterday."

Celeste turns to him. "I heard about that on the news. I heard Kindle Mars used a combination he was not authorized to use, and killed the guy."

The driver nods. He continues, "Yes he set his ass on fire with the Wildfire combination. Death came prematurely to the young thug. The authorities immediately swarmed the place and locked up Kindle." The man looks at me and continues, "Don't be a thug, Mr. Alabaster. Celeste is and has always been the model Blacksmith. If only they all could be like her. Poise and grace, you're an excellent example to live up to Madam Celeste!"

It all sounds condescending to me, but I smile and nod to avoid an issue 100s of feet in the air.

Just hearing this guy speak takes be back to when I was in a class with those White kids who would just hurl any insult at me at whim, because they thought it was ok.

To my shock, Celeste did not challenge him. She even agreed to some of what he said. I feel her grasp my hand and when I turn to her, she winks with a smirk to give me some unspoken reassurance.

After what felt like forever, about 20–25 minutes later, a massive black castle appeared, leaving me awestruck. It was a castle made of black marble that looked like something out of a fairytale.

It was on top of a tiny mountain in the middle of the forest. This, the same forest I partly destroyed. I can see the spot I took out a few miles away. From an aerial view, it definitely looks devastating. The carriage slows down to land on the ground floor.

We landed several feet away from the gate and in front of us were several guards, all dressed in black. Their expressions were mute, and they just stared unflinchingly into whatever was in front of them. They all had a balled fist grasped by their other hand which they pleasantly positioned in front of their bodies near their lower abdomen.

However, I noticed, none of them had a keychain on their wrists. Interesting.

They looked like they were ready for anything, but their calm demeanor was unsettling. "Well, here is your stop. Come again, you two," Talon says, his hand extended, showing his palm.

Celeste drops 2 tokens in his hand and opens the door.

"Just 2, Madam Celeste?" he asks.

She replies, "Yes, I wanted to tip you 1 too. See you later, Talon."

We both exit the carriage and he snarls before promptly flailing the carriage back into the air. I stand still and allow the wind to breeze through my afro. From this ascended view, I can see the vast valleys in the forest. I get a good sense of the environment. A pause of reflection ensues.

"On top of a miniature mountain and in front of a huge gated castle, this is definitely not what I expected," I murmur. "You sure we don't need to make a reservation first, Celeste? These guards look like they mean business." I was slightly shaken.

"Absolutely not, my dear. Come," she insists, and we both walk toward the gate. The men don't break their stare to even acknowledge us. "Hello gentlemen, we are here to see Grandlock Albedo. He is expecting this young one here," Celeste says, but to no response. None of the guards respond.

"EXCUSE ME. This young male has an appointment with the Grandlock."

Again, no one responds to her. She approaches the gate's handle and touches it. A guard points his index and middle finger toward her face.

With a red glow swirling on his fingertips, he warned, "Step back, or I'll blow your brains out." I stood frozen. Should I help her? Celeste's composure is unwavering.

The guard suddenly looks shocked. Several of them share the same facial expression. I can hear a tiny audio of what must be a voice.

A device becomes visible as the guard moves his hand to his ear.

"Are you sure, Grandlock? I didn't see anyone on your schedule today. Okay, if you say so." The guard turns to us after having this conversation.

All the guards look shaken.

"You both may enter. This way ma'am. I apologize for that, and do ask for your forgiveness," the guard says.

Celeste happily trots through the gate, and I hesitate. Something feels odd. It's almost like I can somewhat recognize this place, but I don't know why. "Ashe, come," Celeste commands.

I close my eyes and say a soft prayer. "Lord, wherever I am entering, please be with me." I open my eyes and walk through the gate.

Entering the garden, the gate slams shut. As I turn around, all the guards look at me through the gate as though they saw a phantom just walk in.

Alabaster's True Heritage

Walking through the garden, I noticed the greenery was immaculate. The scene featured fresh shrubs and beautiful statues, all without blemish or decay. It was a pleasant scene to witness, and the atmosphere put me in an extravagant mood. When Celeste and I get to the entrance, I gasp at how tall the doors are.

Someone twelve feet tall could effortlessly walk through. "Is this really happening?" I whispered. Something about this place felt all too familiar, as if from a dream.

This further bolstering my theory that this all cannot be real. But it's best to play along since Mr. "Grandlock" seems to be all knowing. He should be able to tell me how to get home, therefore. The inside of the castle looks like what you'd imagine if watching a show about a celebrity's mansion.

The hardwood floor has smoke grey coloring and is without an itch of dirt. The same applies to the various paintings, murals, and sculptures. There were a variety of different stairs that look as though they could lead to several places. One striking feature was a long, winding staircase that seemed to ascend endlessly.

* * *

"See Ashe, they don't just build this kind of design for just anyone. Only the most worthy of the most high honors in the world gets this special treatment," Celeste says. Amid her showcasing the scene, I look over at a man trying to get our attention.

He was an aesthetically Asian man, I would say, with blue eyes and a blonde afro. He carried a jar of water and gestured to us the offering.

I wave him away. "No thank you, sir." On the other side of the room was another man gesturing with his hands to come to him. He dressed in all black and looked aesthetically Black.

He dawned a smile and gestured to follow him. "Come sir, Albedo has been expecting you both." We both turn to him and walk toward the stairs, the spiraling ones to be exact. We embark on this journey upward toward what seemed like a never-ending path.

Visibly, you can see me zone out into inner reflection. I always find myself here. As time has gone on, I continue to put the pieces of the life I once had back together and am still wanting. I feel so out of place, yet I've always felt out of place. I need to know how I got here and this Grandlock is supposed to have all the answers.

The stairs winded and winded to the point where I got dizzy.

Madam Celeste kept a steady pace as did this guide, but I couldn't tell if I was tired of walking or the anticipation made me tired of waiting. I truly need this to be the final act in this intricate play. What if this Grandlock doesn't like me?

What if he cannot help me get home?

What if this Grandlock truly plotted on this exact moment in time to kill me, because he didn't want to be challenged by someone with the same ability to use black HUE as he?

I don't think the latter is a preposterous position to take. This guy knew I existed this entire time and never once reached out to so much as to say "Hi." This can only mean he strategically waited for me to show up. Admittedly, I am not impressed by the jarring idea of something other than God being omniscient, because it just doesn't seem legit. So whatever crafted dream this is, no matter what the response is, I intend to put an end to this RIGHT NOW.

Someone somewhere must be controlling this simulation, because there is NO WAY!

Or could this be a very vivid dream?

Afterward, I will awaken in my room and likely forget 2/3 of this feature length fantasy. Then the question will become, was it worth it? Was all this unwanted stress worth not even remembering the goal and intent?

We almost reach the end of the steps and I grow even more anxious. "Madam Celeste, do you believe this place would be equivalent to the seven wonders of the world from my time, to Aethereans of this time?"

She smiles and then answers, "I would say yes and no. The seven built wonders, perhaps. Natural wonders in you all's time were important because humans of your time had no genuine connection to the natural world, which amplified something so beautiful to them. Nowadays, Huemans' souls are intricately woven into nature. The 'wonders' are now the individual."

She pauses and gazes into my eyes. "Ashe, you are the wonder. Huemans resoundingly will agree, in due time. Remember this, right now you and Grandlock Albedo are the only two in the world to have a sprightly Black

Key."

The Black Key being the most powerful Key in existence and being in my grasp is still so undeserving. However, I learned never to look a gift horse in the mouth. I am grateful to God for giving me this gift to experience, whether this is the real thing or not. God gave me this experience for a reason.

The final set of steps arrived and I could almost jump to kiss the floor. The upstairs contains several rooms down a decorative hall. This hallway was rather spacious and even boasted a tall ceiling from which the biggest chandelier I have ever seen hung.

Glistening metallic stones in distinct colors—red, brown, gold, green, blue, violet, and black—composed it. "It is just down this hallway. We are almost there," the guide says. He had not broken a sweat yet in this entire process. Nearing a room at the end of this elongated hallway, we pass by so many pictures.

Some of which were depictions of humans holding hands, a meteor striking the Earth, society coming to behold the seven Keys, etc. These pictures were very interesting takes on the history Celeste espoused previously. Interestingly, there was one portrait in particular that showed a boy with all seven Keys above him and several people, including adults, falling to their knees to worship him.

We get to the room's entrance and it didn't look any different from any of the other doors. I must admit, there was an ominous feeling that suddenly came over me.

I couldn't decipher if it was because of my anxiety and anticipation. As Celeste and I continued walking, I realized our guide had stopped. We stood before him as he held a position of attention.

* * *

"You all are welcome to enter." He bid a good day and departed.

Before I could get my mind ready, Celeste knocks on the door. *KNOCK, KNOCK.* We get no response.

She knocks again. *KNOCK.* "Maybe we should just walk in?" Celeste ponders. She tries to open the door. It would not budge. She was becoming visibly irate.

"Allow me, Celeste."

I grab the door by its handle. I turn it slightly and the knob twists. The door opens to my amazement and Celeste's irritation.

She softened her expression, however. I think she may have been more anxious than I to see this Grandlock. "You first, madam." I gesture politely with my hands and she walks into the room.

"Thank you, gentleman," she says. We both walk in and it was like walking into a new world. I'm looking at a spacious, dimly lit room. Its ceiling is framed with gems that give it a star-like quality.

I couldn't help but look around slowly, basking in all the beauty in the room. On the walls were so many paintings. One caught my attention, particularly. It held seven members with different colored eyes, surrounding Earth. Earth had the Pangaea look-alike, so I knew this was in reference to something modern.

"Those are Medley's seven Warlocks, Ashe," Celeste says from behind me.

"They hold executive authority over all laws and rules that reach their desk. The middle one here, with the grey eyes, is the Grandlock Albedo, himself.

The remaining six Warlocks, each from a different noble family, aid in establishing the rule of law."

Celeste has to hold herself back from touching the portrait. "Medley, thus the world, has an aristocratic government. Six of the seven families run the world and hold positions in all the towns' governing bodies. These six families always serve as Warlocks, and a skeleton born with that unique condition fills the seventh role."

Each of the seven Warlocks sports a black robe and white neck stripe.

As I looked at them, I reflected, "It's wonderful that they're from such varied cultural backgrounds. She's Black, he's White." I then pause having remembered, there is no such thing as White in this time period.

Instead, it's all by eye color. I see instead someone with red eyes, brown, gold, green, blue, violet, and of course, grey for the Grandlock. Not one black-eyed person like me and Madam Celeste in sight.

"So Celeste, if they determine the laws to be valid or not, who actually writes them?" I ask.

"Every town also has special councils from each district. They are community based. Problem is, the Warlocks only look at laws from their own communities. It is deeper than just their eye color. With that being said, most of these Warlocks from around the world come from well-established neighborhoods, which is not the case for most Black Locks. So, our laws are vastly underrepresented."

Celeste sighs. "I used to be on one of these councils 100s of years ago, but when I finally accepted that the aristocratic government with Albedo and the other six would never bend to the wishes of the south side, I lost hope."

* * *

"Oh, Celeste, don't demonize me so unsightly," says a voice from behind us. I turn to find a tall, slender man with olive skin like me and eyes grey as a stormy cloud.

"Grandlock Albedo?! It is my pleasure to see you once again," says Celeste in an awe. She slightly bows her head respectfully.

His face was of an antique quality, but not nearly of a person you'd expect to have been around as long as Celeste claims he has been. He steps forward and I can feel my stomach knot up. "So you're the Gran.. Grand.." I struggle to even get the words out of my mouth.

"Yes, I am indeed the Grandlock. I am one of the seven Warlocks of Medley. It is my pleasure to meet you." He extends his hand to me. We shake hands briefly.

His grin was from ear to ear. A feeling of safety slowly eases my anxiety. He dawned a black tie and grey button down blazer. I almost would liken him to be dressed for a wedding. Noticeably, the top of his head of hair is black and wavy, while the sides are grey. His eyes pierced through me and I stood still, frozen. "Your eyes are truly the blackest of all the Locks in Aether," he acknowledges. Interestingly, his eyes were most intriguing to me.

"Your eyes, they are grey."

"Yes young Lock, all skeletons have grey eyes," he replies.

I struggle to put my thoughts together to ask him a question. His presence was shrinking to my ego because he seemed as though he radiated confidence, and perhaps expected it from me.

* * *

I couldn't fake that if I wanted to. Instead, I stood there partially smiling up at him. "Celeste, I understand the plight of the Black Locks in town. Truly, I do. I have always respected you as the model Lock, no matter the color."

She blushes at his words. Her smile had never been that bashful since I had been around.

"Mr. Albedo, I don't mean to be so forthcoming but I simply want answers. Why am I here? You're the only other person on this planet with this Void Key that can use it, right? You're omniscient, correct? Did you send for me?"

I fired so many questions his way it was no wonder he reacted with a prolonged stare. His face had a mute expression. Even Celeste looked a bit bewildered at my line of questioning, but amused. She giggles slightly behind me.

Turning, Albedo heads for a rolling chair. Settling down, he takes a sip of what I assume is coffee.

"Come. I want both of you to come over and let's talk," he insists. I look toward Celeste and she already has started walking toward him. So, I follow suit. The dimlit atmosphere created an ominous vibe. It almost felt like these black walls were going to take a life of their own and close in on me.

We make it to Albedo's chair. A glass desk sat behind him with his cup sitting on top. I look closely and see a black powdery substance sitting next to the cup in a straight line.

"So Ashe, you will forgive me for this, but I will be answering all of those questions altogether to avoid wasting too much of your time. Someone as important as you shouldn't waste their time with an old Warlock like me," he said.

* * *

I noticed he moved his chair to the side to cover the view of the cup and the line. The door opens and all eyes turn to an East Asian phenotypically looking man with his face looking in worry. He rushes to Albedo dressed in a suit and tie, while the door closes slowly behind his entrance. "Master Albedo, you will forgive me."

Sweat falls from his forehead. His glasses grow a foggy film on them and he cleans them immediately to see. "I always tell you Storm, don't worry about being late. But I know it's your lot in life to worry, so be it," Albedo responds in a calm tone.

This man, Storm, turns to me. He looks like he sees a monster from a different realm.

"Oh my HUE, you truly exist? I had to see it for my own eyes to believe it," he says. I don't know whether this is a flattering read on me.

"Storm, your timing is perfect. I want you to perform a scan on him and document how many HUEs you see. Then do the same with his family history," Albedo commands.

Without hesitation, Storm walks toward me. I slowly back away.

"Don't be nervous, Ashe. This is a standard procedure done on those who recently discover their Keys," Celeste assures.

I feel a tad more comfortable. He comes closer, his gaze is as if peering into my soul. He closes his eyes for an extended period. Before opening them, he waits, and then, "Unlock. 2.. 3, 4... 7."

He writes it all down.

* * *

His voice crackles when saying, "He—has . . . seven black HUEs, Albedo." A withering plant could have more life in its speech patterns compared to this worrisome man.

His mood calms after he takes a deep breath. "Young man, would you like to join me and take a look at your padlock? I am using a special combination that only the Goldenrod family knows that allows me to see all of your spiritual inner workings. But, you don't need a combination to look at your padlock."

I hesitate to respond to him. "I wouldn't mind sir, . . . but I don't know how to see my padlock."

He smiles. "Just close your eyes. Think about the safest place you feel and it will appear."

Unfortunately, seeing all the darkness I see when I close my eyes doesn't make a melanophobic person per se, "feel safe."

I try it, anyway. I try to think about what makes me feel the safest. A memory shrouds me and I see a vision of a woman cradling me as a white-haired baby in her arms. This was unintended and unintelligible to me where it came from, but after seeing it for a moment, I feel safe. I dive deep into my body. Deeper and deeper to the point, it felt like I was looking at a galaxy full of stars as I sailed through in a spacecraft.

I force my way through the darkness, trying not to tremble, and it's like I come to a complete stop. Before me was what looked like an actual combination lock, complete with an arrow and numbered in a circle of 0 to 100. The dial was a triangular arrow that was positioned and pointing at the 0. "You see that, young sir? That's your padlock," Storm says. He continued, "Only you and your lineage possess this unique item."

The HUE: Red Part 1

"My lineage? You can see my lineage from my padlock?"

Storm shakes his head and laughs. "Well, sort of!" He then moves to an unacknowledged side of the room that had a large scale computer. It was in the dark, which is why I think it escaped my sight. Albedo nonchalantly clasps his hands and moves from left to right in his wheeled seat in visible contemplation.

His expression almost implied he was curious too, which is strange. Isn't this guy supposed to be "all-knowing?" Storm types something into this jumbo sized computer and the silence in the room made every button pressed echo.

"Please, come here young male," Storm commands. Celeste cheerfully nudges my back, thus I walk toward him. He holds his hand out and I infer he wanted me to place my hand under his.

He positions my palm on a specific dark and shaded area on the machine. "Now, exert your HUE into the computer," he insists. A bit of confusion causes me to freeze. I hadn't mastered this HUE thing, and I didn't know how to produce it. A flashback of that dome destroying the forest came over me. WHAT IF THAT HAPPENS AGAIN?

Storm, noticing, said, "Don't worry, please release your HUE."

I take a deep sigh. With my eyes shut, I feel a rush of black energy coursing through me into the machine via my hand. Immediately, you can see Storm's eyes light up in wonder. The computer screen's 3D effect was so realistic, it felt like a virtual world.

It looked like the stars spiraling in a black cosmos and then a perfect image with words appeared high on the screen. Everyone in the room looks up at it. I opened my eyes wide to get a better look. Grandlock Albedo, in the background, rises to his feet at the screen's message:

LINEAGE: BLACK FAMILY.

BORN: THE 53th DAY OF THE BLACK MONTH YEAR 3004.

PLACE OF BIRTH: UNDETERMINE.

GENETIC ANCESTRY: MOTHER'S SIDE

I snatch my hand away from the machine. "What is this machine talking about? 3004? It was just 2023!" I say with indignation.

Storm leans closer to the information. He adjusts his glasses as though to reread it. "Alabaster Black, it would seem that this is your true heritage. Tracing the Black family back to the beginnings of huemankind reveals their noble heritage."

My eyes penetrate his. "What makes my heritage noble?"

"Nobles are Locks who belong to a family that has seven HUEs of one color. These families are the oldest in Medley and the oldest in the world." Celeste says.

"See Mr. Black, your Key is always determined by the family member that has the most HUEs," Storm says. "So for example, a woman with seven blue HUEs has a child with a man with four blue HUEs: the child will take after the maternal lineage's Key with a seven blue HUE count. Trust me, it's not that complicated. Just remember this: more HUE means more power."

"It is the most perfect the Key can ever be when it has a seven HUE count,"

Albedo chimes in.

Storm places his hand hesitantly on my shoulder. Like seriously, I can see it trembling while he gently holds me. "Mr. Black, wherever you were from, you indeed belong here in Aether. Welcome."

I struggle away from him, "Ashe! Respectfully, my name is Alabaster Ashe. I do not know what this is, but whatever wacky experiment is being played on me needs to cease now!"

I spin around, looking in every direction as if to be breaking some fourth wall that existed.

Storm looks on to me shook, while Celeste hid her head in her palm and just shook it in shame. "ASHE, you said your name was? So be it," says Albedo. The Grandlock had been relatively silent this entire exchange, and now all eyes fell on him.

Something about this dude is off-putting and I'm not sure what. WAIT A SEC. "Grandlock Albedo, are you truly omniscient?"

Celeste gasps, "Ashe stop it! This is Grandlock Albedo you are talking to! I apologize Albedo, sir. He did not mean it." Albedo's bland expression had not bulged.

He sits back down and directs the two of us to come in closer.

"Ashe, truthfully, I didn't expect your arrival. Since the day you showed up and destroyed the Arcane forest, I have lost my omniscience." The entire room looked stunned.

Celeste couldn't help but scream. I turn to comfort her with a hug. "Wait

Albedo, what does that mean for the safety of Aether if you do not possess the ability to see present facing issues and stop crime? Who will predict natural disasters?" she asks.

"There is a small circle of people who are on a need to know basis, dear Celeste. By small, I am referring to the other Medley Warlocks, Storm, you all, and myself. If anyone else were to know, it would be easy for me to pinpoint the culprit," he says calmly with a smirk.

"So, you'll operate based on a Santa Claus-like reputation?"

Grandlock Albedo found it humorous. "Actually, yes Ashe. The mere name of me will cause at least seven billion people to second guess committing a crime. As far as weather, now Celeste, you know we have specialized Locks who handle that."

An awkward silence befell us. By the expression on Celeste's face, she was not truly ready to accept this. I stand fixed in my head. "Grandlock, please tell me you know of some kind of way I could've been from the future and the past at the same time."

Albedo slightly turns left and right in his wheeled chair in a contemplative manner. What caught my eye again was that thick black powder behind him in a line next to his cup. "Ashe, the simplest explanation is that a Black Key possessor sent you back in time to be raised there. Like a ticking time bomb, your Key finally exposed itself to you and well, here you are.

"A force propelled you 1,000 years into the past, and you subsequently journeyed almost 2,000 years into your future. Question is, who?"

Now, I can admit that made sense. There could've been a combination that some Locksmith, maybe my mom, could have gained that would have allowed her to do everything he was talking about. I stare at my keychain and stare hard at the one black colored triangle with the numbers.

"Grandlock Albedo, how would someone have learned such a technique? Wouldn't there have to be some kind of list or instructions to using these Keys?"

"Yes, that is called a 'combination book.' Everyone has one. But at that time, the Black Key was abundant and useful. It was not a vestigial Key. So, combination books for your particular Key would've been common. They are no longer in existence and have not been for centuries. My book, the Skeleton Combination book, has combos for the Black Key, but the rest do not. Reason being, I have been alive since the Black Key was functioning.

"But this is no longer the case and even I don't have the combinations to time travel."

He extends his right hand. I shake his hand with mine and our keychains touch. Mine black and looking like a cosmos, his multicolored and looking like a rainbow in a lava lamp. I pause, then slowly retract my hand. I ball my fist because it just sounds like every answer leads to a dead end and nothing leads me back to home.

"Ashe, I wanted to have you here because I wanted to tell you that we are considering a very important change that you and Celeste must promise not to tell," Albedo says in a serious tone. Celeste and I both nod in agreement.

"For the first time in centuries, the Warlocks and I will consider stepping down, allowing a new generation of Locks to take to power in Aether. They will govern accordingly and will establish laws and practices that all of Aether must follow—because Medley is the beacon of the world.

* * *

"What we put into law will affect every town on this planet. Right now, a requirement in order to be considered in this aristocratic governance is to be of a noble family. Just as I thought, that seems to include you, Ashe."

My eyes widen enormously. "We are considering stepping down and allowing the election of a fresh crop of young people to govern. Being the only one of your respective noble family, would automatically qualify you. Thus, you would take over MY role. Does that sound interesting?"

My heart felt like it skipped a beat. "I mean, I do not know."

"This would give you the opportunity to be mentored by me and I could allow for the use of my combination book to help you unlock your potential," Albedo says.

I don't see any avenues outside of his proposal to learn how to tame this Key. However, I am not just going to jump into it. "Well Grandlock, I don't want to overwhelm him. Maybe he and I will go home and discuss this, first. He may need a proper explanation and to rest on an answer," Celeste says in a hurried speech pattern. I noticed she was in awe and excitement once Albedo mentioned me being mentored by him.

"Well, tomorrow I will be having a special council in the middle of the town. By then, it would behoove of Ashe to have an answer," Albedo instructs, looking serious. Albedo finishes with a hug to Celeste, followed by a handshake to myself. The handshake was a long one. I could swear I saw black HUE on his palms for a brief moment.

As we walk out, Storm's nervousness continues to shroud the atmosphere.

"Have.. a nice night, you two," he stutters, as we walk past him.

* * *

"You too, Storm," we both say in unison.

"Oh and Ashe, don't let what happened in the forest happen again. No one needs to know you have an active Black Key until at least tomorrow night. I will present you onstage in front of the townsfolk and the other Warlocks. So, try your best to stay out of trouble." Albedo says. He delivers a final goodbye wave.

Hand on my back, Celeste and I departed.

The door slams and the men stare at each other. Albedo turns around to his coffee cup. A spoon next to it is used to scoop half of that thick black line into the liquid and stir it. He sips before deciding to scoop the other half.

"You know WHAT I saw Albedo," Storm says. Albedo takes another sip calmly as if he ignored him. "ALBEDO! This is a dangerous game to play! Why would you tell him about your lack of omniscience?!"

Albedo looks up momentarily, then at Storm.

"It was no sense in hiding it. Why would we perform all of this if I knew everything? Now pass me my combination book so I can refresh on a combo that will allow me to have some form of foresight. As long as I can predict the future, I will be a step ahead. I want you to phone all the Warlocks and tell them to come to my lair for an emergency meeting right now. Anyone who is not compliant will be at risk of death. We have to catch it this time, before history is to repeat itself," Albedo ends.

Black versus Nonblack

"Wait, so your name is Alabaster Black?" Jasper asks innocently.

"Yes," I replied, "but I'd rather you call me, Ashe." I sit with my head down next to Jasper as he asks question after question, despite my relative silence. Celeste and Eve sit on the couch perpendicular from the one we sat.

Eve's eyes looked a bit concerned, trying to gather what all had gone down at the Grandlock's estate. Meanwhile, the scheduling of me for a "Warlock" role seemed to fill Celeste with confidence and joy. I honestly couldn't care less. I felt sad because my journey to this world's "grand wizard" yielded more questions than answers.

"So Ashe, you really were born here, in this time then? Or was it at an earlier time? But NOT in your time? I am confused," Eve said what I'm sure everyone else was thinking. The sad part was I couldn't even explain it.

"Alabaster was born in 3004 to a woman who must've had an active Black Key. She sent him to the past to be raised by ancient humans in the 21st century. His Key awakens and BOOM—he's here at the start of the year 4003. It's simple as that," Celeste states. It just didn't feel that simple. Nowhere in my memory bank can explain how years of living in Alabama, I just vanish one day and wake up here.

NOTHING.

I can't even remember what I was doing before this all transpired. I woke up in school clothes though, so I must've been going to class when something happened. Could the Key have awakened in the middle of class? That's got to be some drama for the news.

"Ashe—" Celeste calls and interrupts me in deep thought.

"You will forgive me for telling your special news, but he is going to be chosen to be an intern of Albedo. Grandlock said that Ashe might be taking over his role as Head Warlock!"

Eve and Jasper both gasp.

Both riddle with confusion. Meanwhile, the role's gravity escaped me. "They are actually considering a different Warlock council? Oh, my word? No one has done that in hundreds of years," Eve says.

"He just got here! I doubt he even knows what it takes to be a Warlock!" exclaims Jasper.

"Hush, you all! Don't you see the magnitude of this offer? If Ashe becomes Grandlock, he'd be the first Lock from the south side district and FIRST BLACK LOCK to represent us. There's power in that." Everyone takes a moment to reflect on Celeste's words.

"Celeste, I truly apologize for such foolish thinking. You are so correct. Ashe, I wish for you the best on this venture," Eve says warmly. A look into her gorgeous golden eyes confirmed her warm intentions.

* * *

"I apologize as well, Ashe. If the highest authority in the world says you're a viable candidate for Warlock, then that means you are." Jasper smiles up at me on the couch.

Celeste turns to Eve. "This is also an opportunity for you, Eve. You are a Goldsmith from a noble family. Seven gold HUEs means you might get a vote cast for yourself."

Eve sits with a smile and a soft blush. I could tell there was a slight discomfort in what Celeste tried to envision for her. "Well to be honest, Ashe, you don't know this, but I am a part of a group that has been calling for the egregious aristocratic governance to be done away with. While Albedo stepping down and allowing a Black Lock to takeover is progressive, I would say it still being aristocratic is troubling to me."

Eve's words were like a symphony in my ear. I could listen to this girl talk forever. "Eve, do not let this opportunity escape you over pride, my dear. The world operates this way whether you like it or not. If you get in the door, then maybe you can make a change from the inside," Celeste says. Eve turns to our direction on the other couch.

"Jasper, what do you think?" she asks.

"Eve, I'll have to give that some thought. I see both sides of you all's views. I would agree that this is a tremendous opportunity for you, Eve, but I also think the aristocratic governance is chaotic and just not modern enough for the start of the year 4003," he responded.

Silence befell the room. A simple look at me could tell I was slightly overwhelmed with it all.

* * *

"Ashe, I know that this is all moving fast for you, but it is a good thing. This is a great thing. Every Lock in the world, at some point, wants to be a Warlock," Celeste says comfortingly.

Eve looks at Celeste as if a lightbulb went off in her head. "Wait Madam Celeste, does this mean you are considering rejoining this district's council to write laws?" she asks. Celeste nods.

"Yes. I will reapply first thing in the morning. I know there are plenty of vacancies in this district. Ashe's nomination will motivate some discouraged Locks to become active and make a difference!" Celeste says passionately.

I would be lying if I said I wasn't a tad bit excited as well.

I'm not excited about the glory of the nomination, but genuinely curious. How does becoming an understudy to the most sovereign being on the planet feel like? That's curiously daunting to me, to be honest.

But then I see my white afro and pitch black irises in the mirror on the wall. That's when reality sets back in. Not this guy! Not the guy who is scared of his own HUE. He's going to be leading the masses on this futuristic planet?

Please!

I doubt that. I'm sure, right before my inauguration, I'll do something unconventionally stupid and get the title stripped before it's given. In a world where I have nothing but questions and no answers, however, I think it's best I go with the flow. "Whatever the results are tomorrow Celeste, I will be grateful."

"That's the attitude I want to hear!" she says.

* * *

Eve jumps to her feet. "I almost forgot I have to run to the store and get this last item to make dinner."

Eve acts frantically and pulls out a rectangular piece of small paper. It showed crossed-out ingredients.

"The market ran out of asparagus an hour ago, but they should be restocked now. Let me run to the store really quick," she says. She throws on her coat that hung in the closet. She then looks around and finds her shoes across the room.

She flicks her hand in the shoes' direction, exclaiming, "Unlock!" A stream of elastic lightning flows from her golden HUE, snatches the shoes off the ground, and brings them to her palm. The gold HUE disperses and slowly disappears. I look amazed.

"That was brilliant." My murmuring puts a smile on Eve's face.

"Oh, it's just a little trick, Ashe." Her humility attracts me to her more. She looks around once more to check that she had not forgotten anything. "Awe, my keychain! I definitely can't go outside without that," she says. The keychain laid flat on top of a book lying on the shelf. I noticed the book was titled "The HUE: Gold."

She points her hand in its direction. "Unlock!" The keychain and the book both are snatched by the lightning. They flail in the air for her to catch. The keychain is caught, but the book falls to the ground. She places the keychain on and immediately the jewel in the center turns gold. All the white triangles spin until they change to golden.

She had a considerable amount of gold triangles.

* * *

"Would anyone like anything additional from the store?" She looked around for answers, but we all shake "no" in unison. "Okie dokie! I will be right back." She walks toward the door.

I yell, "Wait Eve, watch out!" It was too late. Eve steps on the book and slips off of it. She falls to her hip and straddles her right ankle.

"OWW! OUCH, OUCH!"

Celeste and I are the first on the scene. I try to help her rise on her left foot, the good one, and Celeste took over the right side, with the injured foot risen. We limp her to the sofa and rest her.

"Are you ok, Eve?" I ask, leaning in. She smirks as if to hold back a frown.

"Yes, I am ok." Celeste runs to the kitchen to find her footstool. She brings it back and Eve sits her right foot on top. Jasper slides on his knees across the floor toward her foot.

"Don't worry Eve, the Brown Lock is here to save the day," he says in all seriousness. He told me to remove her sock and shoe. I pulled off her shoe and then her sock, exposing her tiny delicate foot. I fight to stay focused, reminding myself that she is suffering terribly. He pulls a small container from his pocket.

When opened, it appeared to be a vial of grey clay. He uses two fingers on both hands to meticulously and slowly bathe her foot all around in the clay. When finished, he closed the tiny container and placed it back in his pocket.

"Ok, this might sting for a second," Jasper says, hovering his hands over her clay covered ankle. "Hippocratic, unlock!" The brown HUE shrouds the foot and when it dissipates, it shows a hardened cast made of clay on Eve's foot.

The cast covered nearly all of her foot and ankle, exposing only her toes.

Jasper was right about the instant pain Eve felt when he called the combination, but she frowned about it only briefly. "I'd say by the morning your foot should be operable as it was," Jasper assures her.

Eve leans in and gives him a hug, followed by a kiss on the forehead. "Thank you, Jasper," she says. The little boy blushes so red I almost forgot he had freckles. Celeste smiles and turns to us.

"Well since Eve will be on bedrest tonight, the responsibility to go retrieve the asparagus falls on you two. Hurry now! It's almost curfew, Jasper. You know the way and Ashe will accompany you for future reference."

We both hop up and put on our respective coats and shoes. Eve hands the list to Jasper (though it felt unneeded) and we both wave before heading out the door. Before I make it fully outside, Celeste has a request. "One more thing, Ashe. Remember what Albedo instructed you: DO NOT DRAW ATTENTION TO YOUR KEY."

I nod in agreement, and we walk out of the door.

The beautiful night sky offered a nice aesthetic on the quiet sidewalk as we headed to the store. The brisk night with a faint chilly breeze ushered in a calm mood throughout my body. Jasper stepped side by side with me and at some points in the walk I could tell he was politely mimicking my steps. He was trying not to get too far ahead or behind me.

I laughed when I realized and slowed my pace down. I'm sure his tiny legs will thank me later. Walking past all these homes with unique designs, I almost think they look kind of like the ones at home, just with a slight futuristic spin. Mailboxes with last names like "Sepia," "Maroon" and "Cerulean" were interesting sightings. Despite a nice sized street next to us, I had yet to see a car literally anywhere. No garages on these houses were telling as well.

"So cars do not exist in this time period at all?" I ask.

Jasper earnestly responds, "No. Those things harm the environment, so they got rid of them in the year 2086 or something."

"So why is there a street then, little buddy?"

Jasper points to tiny skid marks in the street. "Locks still use carriages and bikes to travel. Those don't harm the environment, they just leave a few marks. Nothing the Brown Locks who street clean can't fix."

I slowly put the pieces of the puzzle together in my head. "Celeste told me that certain Locks go against their family's heritage and join other Houses. What exactly are the requirements to join a House?"

"Locks just have to have the right number of HUEs. Eve, for example, has seven HUEs. That's the maximum anyone can have. Thus, she can join almost any House that takes gold HUE. I, on the other hand, only have two brown HUEs and one black, vestigial HUE. So, I am limited."

"Well, that's unfair, isn't it? I thought this was a 'balanced' world."

Jasper shakes his head. "But see, people would say that's what makes it balanced!" He states, "I can't possibly be expected to carry the street cleaning workload with only two brown HUEs."

* * *

"Oh, why not?"

"HUE runs out and can take one or sometimes two or three days to recharge. In a world where everyone can fight and burn down buildings with no technology, it's safe to say that no one wants to be left HUE-less for too long. So, society is set up a certain way with good intentions, I think."

Jasper turns to me and whispers slightly, "But don't tell Eve I said that. Pinky promise." I laugh, but agree with my pinky.

"You know, I think it may have escaped me, but does Celeste have a Key?"

Jasper looked stunned. "Well Ashe, everyone HAS a Key, but you're wondering about her HUEs. They're all black, vestigial black. She comes from a time where the Black Key was going through a transition and lost its luster, if you will. I think her generation was a part of that first group that was born with only vestigial Keys, which is rare nowadays."

I gasped because I had not even noticed what her keychain's jewel looked like. "Yeah, she has six black HUEs and is kind of sensitive about it, so I would not bring it up." Jasper says.

"Thanks for telling me. I reckon I will not bring that up, little buddy."

Jasper laughs. "Your accent is kind of funny. Does everyone from the past talk like that? Or like just your part?"

"Honestly, I never experienced different people til I came here. I would say, where I come from, my speech is not special or uncommon."

Jasper stops to tie his shoe before we continue to walk. "Let me ask you, what exactly makes someone a Black Lock? Why are these Huemans differentiated from the others so overtly?" Jasper takes a moment before answering.

"Black Locks form when a person has more black HUEs than any other color.

"Remember, you can only have up to seven Keys, thus, only seven HUEs. Secondly, the black HUE differs from others because it defies the rules of nature set for the other six. Let me give you an example:

"If a male with four blue HUEs and a female with three blue HUEs have a child, their kid will have the father's HUE count, because he has the most HUE.

"If a male with four blue HUEs and a female with three red HUEs have a child, their child will have three black HUEs and one blue HUE, because opposite HUEs cancel each other out.

"Now, if a male with three black HUEs has kids with a female with four green HUEs, the children will have four green and three black HUEs. Numerically, the black HUE complements the design rather than erasing it in that sense.

"Black HUE only plays the matching game with other black HUE. So a male with four black HUEs and a female with three will have kids that all have four black HUEs. See, it's that not complicated."

Jasper looks me closely in the eye. "Since the Black Key is conventionally unusable, it is seen as a hindrance. Society, thus, views Black Locks through that lens. Now, Eve and I are exceptions, but most people are not so nice to the Locks with black eyes."

No wonder there is so much riding on me being this Warlock pick. Even if only one of my HUEs were active, that would be enough to give hope to a disparaged group of people. "Let's be clear, Ashe. I still stand with the plight of the Blacksmiths. My mom died young and my father never was in my life, so Celeste adopting me at the age of five showed how society treats Blacks differently. I've known since my earliest years that I was privileged."

While walking, Jasper's eyes soften when he looks at me. "Word of advice, just be careful sort of **pathologizing** the condition of being a Black Lock. From my experience, even though their eyes are black, most would say they identify with the HUE that is active. That is what they would say is their true Key, not the vestigial ones."

I have to admit, I enjoyed listening to Jasper articulate this world to me. Now I have a different perspective on what the real problem is. If Albedo knows how this society does this kind of hierarchical prejudice against the Black Locks, why has he not stepped in more?

Celeste said she had lost hope until yesterday that the needs of this district full of Blacksmiths would ever be met.

"One last question, Jasper. If Celeste has all vestigial Keys, why is she allowed to be an instructor? What could she teach someone like Eve who has seven active gold HUEs?"

"Every House has a book. You saw Eve slip on her family's combination book earlier. Now, every House isn't going to let you in. You got to have the right amount of HUEs for it. You got to have the right Key for it.

"But, for Houses that specialize in an archaic subject like Archeology/ Anthropology, they require Albedo's approval. The combinations in those books just expound on the two basic combos every Lock can learn, no matter the color."

"What are those combos?" I murmur to myself. "Celeste said hand-to-hand combat was also part of the training. Is that House specific?"

"Most of us learn at a young age from the community leaders before we progress to learn more from our respective Houses. Since 90% of Locks further their education within their family's House, it's safe to say they will continue their heritage's fighting style as well," he responds.

We arrived in the neighborhood.

I question the safety as the homes looked more and more dilapidated the further we walk. I look to a scenery of rusty swing sets on the playground and trash ridden all around a trashcan.

Teens that look no older than Jasper were forming up and shoot dice in the middle of the sidewalk.

One little boy points his finger and a small spark of electricity spouts to flip each die. "That's 7, I win!" he exclaimed and the other male gave him one of those black tokens.

"Oh, you're so full of shit! Next game we are playing with no combinations," the losing male dictates.

His language surprised me. I continued walking, concealing my shock. My dad would've got a belt for me had I used that language, especially so young.

The general vibe was unkept on this part of town. "Ya know Jasper, I can't say that this level of degradation has changed much from my time period. Only difference is that it's not just the Nonwhite people. Here every race seems to participate in self-destructive behaviors."

"We don't have your racial hierarchy anymore, Ashe. But comparatively,

Blacks are still at the bottom of the totem pole. Just the totem isn't a White to Black one, it is more Black to Nonblack. Black is at the bottom and all Nonblack HUEs are at the top." His tone shift and subtleties of sadness can be heard.

He pats my back in comfort. "I mean, it's not like I have an inspiring HUE set up. I have two brown HUEs and one black one. HA! I barely made it to being a Nonblack Lock."

We approach a store that was well lit.

"The Emerald Market."

Fruit scents filled the air as we entered. Lavish tomatoes, cucumbers, bell pepper, etc. hang on the racks looking the healthiest I ever did see. Strawberries, blueberries and watermelon all are on another side of the room on racks. Here, an elderly man with a generous smile sweeps the remainder of the debris from the floor.

He turns to notice a blemish on a collard's leaf and immediately raises his palm drenched in green HUE. "Unlock," he said, restoring the leaf to its vibrant green. He goes back to sweeping.

"Good-afternoon, Mr. Emerald," Jasper says.

The old man turns and leans in. "Huh? Someone there?"

"It's me, Jasper Bistre, from Celeste's home." He finally raises his face and I get a small glimpse of his greenish eyes.

"OH, Jappy! How are you?" he asks.

* * *

"I am doing just fine. My new roommate and I are looking to buy asparagus if it were no bother."

"Aw a new roommate? This fine young man here? What is your name, young sir?"

I bashfully respond, "Alabaster.. Black.."

"Alabaster? Oh no, I'm fresh out of alabaster mints, but if you give me a sec, I can make you a few," he responds loudly.

"Oh no sir, my name is Alabaster." I say louder.

"OH, your name is Alabaster? Nice. What a fine name."

Jasper giggles. I shake my head.

"Whose doing the cooking tonight, Jappy?"

"Madam Celeste is cooking tonight," he responds.

The old man blushes. "Oh that Madam Celeste, she's a wildcard. I swear she was supposed to be my wife a few 100s of years ago." Jasper and I both halt ourselves from laughing at the revelation.

"If you sit around him long enough, he will tell you plenty of stories," Jasper whispers to me.

Mr. Emerald went to a shelf and plucked the finest array of asparagus. Jasper and I meet him at the register.

"Ok, so usually I can charge 1 token for this, but for you and your friend

Jappy, it'll be for free." He hands the asparagus to us, but Jasper politely shoves it back.

"No, Mr. Emerald. You are the one solid in this entire district that serves the Blacksmiths without prejudice. We want to patronize your business." Jasper follows with a token with the number 1 on it.

We then procure the asparagus and head out.

"See you, Mr. Emerald," Jasper says.

I follow with a wave.

"Okay now! Tell Celeste to come see me sometimes! Also, be careful Japs. There's been a string of thefts taking place out here. I'd hate for you and your friend to get caught up in that. There's a heavy police presence out here cause of it."

We both nod and walk out the door, back into the cold, silent air.

We casually walk back down from where we came.

"He's kind."

"YES. Mr. Emerald is the kindest old man on this side of the southern district. He's been around as long as Celeste and used to be on the council with her. They go way back!"

"That's awesome, Jasper."

* * *

The quiet almost made our steps echo. "Hey, Jasper. What is a 'solid?' You called Mr. Emerald one."

He looks into the air to think before responding. "Oh, a solid is a person who has all HUEs of one color. He has six green HUEs."

I take a moment to reflect. "Why is he in THIS neighborhood? I thought that the more HUEs of one color meant more opportunities and whatnot."

"They do. He just is a kind soul. The south district has 95% Blacksmiths with two or less active Keys. Everyone holds Mr. Emerald as a pillar in this community."

The sight of graffiti everywhere would've been enough for me to move away 100s of years ago. I wonder if at one point the Black Locks lived with dignity and self-respect in their neighborhood.

Something catches my attention out of the side of my eye. I know I saw it, but as I turn . . . it's not there anymore.

It's just a light pole, blinking on and off. I catch my breath. "It's just a light pole." Jasper overhears me. He turns around and sees me quivering in horror.

I take another glance. I blink and a crow has landed on the light. Fear grips me. "So Jasper, I don't know if I got a chance to tell you. I suffer from melanophobia."

Hesitantly, I move backwards. I hadn't taken my eye off this thing the entire time. "Melanophobia? Is that like the fear of the color black? Or dark colors?"

"YES. I am terrified of black objects, especially the living ones like this crow."

* * *

"Well Ashe, don't be afraid. It's just a crow. They are common in this part of Medley, dude."

I don't think I heard anything he said. I just know this bird is close to me and needs to fly off. It raises its wings and lets out a loud caw noise. CAWW. I flinch. Jasper throws a pebble at it and it flies away. Ready to defend myself, I cover my face with my arms. I peek through them to see the bird had flown away. I see it aerially hovering back toward the trees of the forest.

"Thank you, little buddy." I kneel down to give him a hug. He pats my back humorously.

"It was nothing," he says. I rise up and stare at the forest.

"You know, Jasper, I had not realized how close we were to that forest. This is the same one I halfway demolished."

I feel a chill breeze come through. I heard something coming out of the forest.

It sounded like a voice I had heard before, but I was unsure.

The figure exclaims, "There you are!" It was that creature with gray skin from before. I trip in fear as it runs toward me with a menacing grimace.

Its hands, bloodied and looking like claws.

As Jasper attempts to intercept it, the figure kicks him aside. He hits the light pole and a crow lands on his head.

"Jasper!" My scream went unheard. I try to gain my footing, but the monster kneels on my groin and raises above me.

* * *

"Now give me your HUE, Blacksmith!" it commands.

Motionless, I lay facing my end. The demonic figure's cold, black eyes stared back at me. A tear falls from my shaky eye and I feel the cold liquid run down my face to my neck.

Murky Waters

"You ready to die?!" the monster asks.

I lie motionless at the kneel of this creature with horrid grey skin. Gasping for air, it was futile to get a word in. Jasper, on the side of me, moves slightly to regain consciousness.

"Ashe," he whispers.

While on top of me, the monster positioned his bloody hand to swing.

"YOUR HUE IS MINE!" it says with the most horrible grin.

"ASHE, your wrist!" Jasper yells. I take a quick look and remember . . . the combination!

The black triangle had written "5, 60 & 5" in individual corners. I immediately close my eyes and try to see that number wheel I saw at Albedo's place.

"Please God. Please show it to me!" I envision a black shimmering mist that clears to show my padlock. There it was, the number wheel.

* * *

The tiny arrow pointed to 0. "Ok, 5 . . . 60 & 5." I watch the wheel move to 5 clockwise, then turn around pass 0 to 60 counterclockwise and then clockwise again to 5 once more. The monster lowers his arm to strike.

"Ashe, unlock it!" Jasper yells.

My eyes open and I throw up my hands.

"UNLOCK!"

The thunderous call forces black HUE from my body into a shield the size of a tiny building. It surrounds me on every side into a perfect half of a sphere. The force of the shield repels the monster backwards, and then something odd happens. The center of its chest glows in a violet light before it explodes into tiny pieces that all evaporate.

Not a trace remains, except the violet HUE that slowly starts to disappear into the atmosphere.

It was as if the entire ordeal hadn't even happened. Though I'm sure Jasper would disagree. At the sight of my black HUE, even the crow fled, revealing the top of Jasper's head. His head bared an enormous lump on top. I lower my hands and the black HUE slowly disappears in every direction.

I run to help Jasper up off the ground. He leans on me so I could help him to his feet, slowly. "You ok, little buddy?" He nods and a sigh of relief overcomes me.

"That thing that chased me in the forest still found me. I think I remember Phoebe saying something about it being a 'Deadlock.'"

* * *

Jasper stands fully erect and catches his balance. "Yes Ashe, that's a Deadlock. Those things exist because their spirit went wayward before death. Thus, they roam the world seeking to cause havoc unto the living. They always say they want to steal your Key, but the reality is that they cannot. They only know the combinations they knew at the time of death, if I am not mistaken."

"Wait, so they mindlessly roam the world attacking people for their Keys? That's kind of dangerous, isn't it? These things are just greeted like natural occurrences?" I'm certain Jasper can hear the irritability in my tone.

He explained, "They're uncommon, yet a typical Lock, as you proved, will usually suffice. Unless powerful, usually one firm knock in the head or the chest area is enough to destroy them.

"Once defeated, their HUE disappears into the atmosphere, like what the good spirits do when they die."

I gather myself as my adrenaline slowly ceases. I did not expect this monster, this Deadlock, to find me.

"Don't worry, Ashe! Those things live in forests and caves where it's dark, because they fear the light. Generally speaking, the only time they attack people is when the person was someone they knew or the person has a powerful HUE," he says. I find clarity in that last statement.

My major concern is Jasper's head. On closer inspection, I see a trail of blood spewing from the top. "Jasper, your head." I point and he tries to feel for the issue. He pauses at the touch of blood.

"It's ok, Jasper. Let's just get you some help."

* * *

He repeats to himself, "It's ok. It's ok. It's ok."

He almost began to sound as though he was hyperventilating with each sentence.

I try to cover his head with my hand foolishly. Obviously, that doesn't stop the bleeding.

I apply pressure to the wound. "Hey, you! What are you doing to that Brown Lock?" a man calls from behind us. A few yards away, he wastes no time walking over to us and confronting me.

He was dressed in all black, a white belt around his waist, and wore a triangular black hat. He was a heavyset male who I would have identified as White, had this been my time. He dawned a distinct bushy brown mustache.

At a closer glance, his shirt read "Medley Police." So he is a cop. He takes a quick look at me, then at Jasper and then back at me. Something in me just knew he judged me guilty. He continued to stare as if he wanted a confession then and there.

"What the hell did you do to this young Brown Lock, boy?" he asked. The officer approaches me at a slow and cautious pace.

"Oh, no sir, this is my roommate. We were just attacked by a Deadlock." My hands go up as if he had a gun.

"LOWER YOUR HANDS BOY," he says in a commanding tone. I follow with hesitation.

Jasper nudges me to look at him.

* * *

"Clasp your hands like me, Ashe." His hands were clasps and upside down. I do the same.

"That's better. Now where is this Deadlock? I don't see any signs of one."

His shirt read "Brass" at the bottom. His eyes matched, thus I assumed this was his last name. "Answer me!"

"Sir, this is my roommate. We are students at the Celeste House of Archeology," Jasper calmly but clearly answered. "I've already taken care of the Deadlock."

"Finally, someone's talking like he's got some sense," the cop responds, while snidely looking at me. "Old lady Celeste, hmph. That old bitch still hasn't kicked the bucket?"

I clenched my right fist and I could hear my knuckles crack.

The cop's eyes widen.

This seemingly infuriated him. He quickly unfastens his keychain. He points his right index and middle fingers at me. "STAND BACK or I'll blow your damn head off, boy."

I stand too frozen to move. The cop's hands start to emit golden HUE. Jasper hastily stands in front of me and spreads his arms out.

"If you're going to kill, be prepared to take two lives not one."

This little boy's head is still gushing blood and yet he bravely stands before me.

* * *

"Get out of my way, little Lock, or I'll send you back to Celeste in a coffin." Jasper backs up toward me, which causes me to back up too. We both move ever so slowly backwards as the cop approaches us.

"You all really want it to end like this? It's your choice!" he says. We bump into a fountain with a statue of a woman spouting water from her palm. Now we are sandwiched between the fountain with a pool of water and this cop in front of us.

He nears even more fearsome than the Deadlock. We hear a splash of water from behind us, and a small puddle forms in front of us.

I could swear I saw a small amount of blue HUE slowly disappear from the puddle.

The cop steps to us and his right foot submerges in the spill.

He swiftly slips and falls backwards.

He then tries to regain footing and slips forward. This he repeats several times back and forth. Jasper turns around to me and after a nervous pause, we both let out a generous laugh. That last time he tries to stand erect, his legs shake. His face is all scratched up.

His hat fell off, revealing his head, which now has more bruises than Jasper's. He tries to step forward. "You . . . little bastards." Those were his last words before he slipped again, this time HARD.

He falls unconscious and a tiny pool of blood starts to leak from him. Jasper and I just stare at him.

"What should we do, Jasper?"

* * *

He looks around.

"I wonder who embedded a combination in this puddle," he asks. I turn around toward the fountain, and a teen that looked about my age appears from behind the statue.

He straddled it and swung around to the front as if he was dancing with the sculpture.

He positioned himself skillfully enough that no part of his body touched the water below him. He had the stereotypical "balanced look" and faced us with a smirk. "Hello all, no need to thank me. This is just what I do out the kindness of my morality," he says.

The boy was probably a few inches taller than me, making him approximately 6 feet and he had a lean body type. Dressed in a thin sweater and jeans, I could tell from his sleeves he had been diving into the fountain in search of something.

He had a flask tied to his side.

He was about the same color as me, olive, and his hair was more straight than mine. I can tell there was a slight wave to it and brown, although he kept a blue bandana tied around it.

His smile showed the most porcelain teeth, and his eyes were eerily blue. Like the most blue I had ever seen. He jumps off the statue and lands perfectly on the ground.

"Well, how's it going? Put it there, you guys," he says jubilantly, with his fist out. I dap fists with him while Jasper hesitates. But he eventually daps his fist as well.

"Did you save us?"

"Of course!" he responds, almost as though he expected the question. "That derelict of a cop doesn't belong around these parts with those kinds of prejudices. I mean, it's 4003, for goodness' sake! The year just started like a day ago.

"I tell you, if it were up to me, I would only employ the Locks who had love in their hearts for everyone.

"Or hate in their hearts for everyone, because at least then it's still fair. Wherever you are, Albedo, 'Mr. all knowing,' I know you're listening. These are some free suggestions."

He talked so quick, I struggled to keep up.

"Well, you helped save us, so thank you." I turn to Jasper and he seemed slightly creeped out. I pat him on the back and realize that he still is bleeding.

"Oh no Jasper, the blood!"

"Never fear, I got just the fix for it." The boy dips his hands in the fountain's water and holds a palm full.

With blue HUE-stained palms, he approached a flinching Jasper.

"Hippocratic, unlock!" He applies the water to Jasper's head. The water and the HUE conjoin to repair his head. The top of his head looked brand new. Jasper touches the top, and no longer is there any blood falling.

* * *

His face grows ecstatic. "Thank you so much, sir," he replies.

"I think seventeen is too young to be a sir, but you can call me that if you'd like. Most people just call me Finnegan, Finnegan Blue," he says cheerfully to Jasper. He goes and dips his hands in water once more.

"Just in case I forget. Hippocratic, unlock!" The blue HUE is applied to the officer's cranium as well. He looked healed, but still unconscious.

"That should take care of him. Don't worry, he'll wake up sooner or later and we'll be long gone. This combination is quite clever, isn't it?

"Too bad you can heal everyone but yourself with it. It should be called the 'Hypocrite combination,'" he rants.

"Thank you . . . 'Finnegan,' was it?"

He replies, "Yes! Finnegan is correct." I noticed him staring hard at my watch on my left wrist. "That's an awfully nice watch you got there. Where'd you get it from?"

"It was a gift." I reach to shake the cheery hand of Finnegan and he shakes exuberantly back. Silence followed our awkward laughter.

Jasper seems to be kind of over it all. "You ready to go, Ashe? It's getting late. Thirteen year olds have a curfew, you know." He tugged on the bottom of my jacket to get my attention.

"You're right, buddy, and Madam Celeste is probably worried. It was nice meeting you, Finnegan. I hope we can meet up again some day." I begin to walk away. Immediately, I feel another tug on my jacket, from Finnegan this time.

* * *

"Madam Celeste? THE Madam Celeste? As in the first Black Lock to grace the cover of *Balanced* magazine?

"Oh trust me, I have had a lot of alone time with her and that picture of her young!

"She's revolutionary. Not only was she a model, but an activist for the Black Locks' rights." He goes on and on too fast for me to keep up.

"Hey bro, we got to go."

"Wait, Ashe was it? Mind if I call you 'Ashy?' I want to say the night is late for the youngster, but not for you, brother. There are ladies calling your name at this club down the street that just opened. Life is about seizing the opportunities and living in the moment," Finnegan says.

I turn to Jasper in confusion. "I think he is referring to 'Grey City Nightclub.' But you got to be sixteen years old to get in, with an ID. Do you have one of those, Ashe?" Jasper asked that question rhetorically.

"Oh, you don't need an ID. All you need is charm and the look. And looking at you, you got it, man. Balanced skin tone, oval-like face, nose not too wide or thin. You're a chick magnet, Ashy.

"Only thing imbalanced about you is that white afro. Only because it sways a bit too kinky. But it being white makes it neither balanced nor imbalanced. It's got an exotic feel to it."

Oddly, I seriously start to consider his offer. I have never been to a club and I wonder what getting that kind of attention from the ladies could be like. No! I can't be swayed by kind words. Madam Celeste sent us here on a mission, entrusting me to go to the store and come back. I look at Jasper and I know it would be wrong to leave him by himself.

"Ashe, I can't stop you if you want to go party, but I would implore you to be careful." Jasper says, walking off. I reach my hand out.

"Wait, Jasper!"

"It's ok, I know MY way home," he says. He continues to walk away.

I stand stagnant and shamefully begin to get upset because I cannot make up my mind.

"It's okay, Ashy! Everyone on the south side knows where Madam Celeste lives, so I'll get you home! The little tyke knows his way, so no worries. Now, about those ladies.

"I guess I should've asked you. Are you at least sixteen years of age? I can get you in either way, but just curious."

"Yes, Finnegan. I am sixteen years old."

He wraps his arm around the back of my neck and leads me down the sidewalk. "Ok, that's what I want to hear. Let's go get em champ." As we leave the scene, the police officer begins to slowly come to. He rises to his side and places his hand on his throbbing head.

"What in the hell was that?"

Down and around the street, we walked almost two miles. About 30 minutes have passed of this guy nonstop talking. We were walking so long it felt like hours. Finnegan talked about hisself the entire time. I know that he:

*left home at the age of thirteen,

*has traveled ALL over Aether for schooling,

*has only one living relative left in Medley, 'Warlock Blue,' (a member of the Warlock council)

*and loves women of all shades.

We make it down the Street and the sign to the place becomes visible: "Grey City Nightclub."

"So, first time to the club?" Finnegan asks me. I nod yes, but I'm very cautious about this guy's kindness.

I mean, he, like most people, doesn't know Albedo lost his omniscience. So I don't think he would do anything incriminating.

I just get an odd feeling about this guy. Jasper will forgive me, however. I need to explore this world as much as possible. So if hanging with this stranger could lead to some enlightenment that wakes me up from this dream, so be it. I would say that getting this so-called 'attention from the ladies' might be a bit enticing as well.

"I have never been to a club or after school dance to be completely clear, Finnegan." The boy laughs at me.

"Where do they do 'after school' dances, Ashy? Is that like a slang term you Blacksmiths have come up with? Sheesh, you guys never fail to amaze me with your creativity."

"Oh, um, never mind."

As we arrive at the club entrance, a blonde with brunette highlights is comfortably seated. Pale skin and straight mid length hair, she sat on a high chair while scoping through a magazine.

A model with Finnegan and my skin tone was pleasantly posed on the *'Balanced'* magazine cover. The model also had brown, wavy hair. Her face was an oval shape and nose straight. Although slim, her body displayed an hourglass figure, and her eyes were perfectly spaced.

The girl was deeply focused on each page she passed. "I wish my hair would do that," she said in a serious tone. We approach her and she looks at us with the coldest expression. Noticeably, her eyes were black like mine.

"Hello ma'am, we were looking to try out this new club. Hear it's worth all the worldly wonder," Finnegan says. She looks back into her magazine and turns the page.

"I need to see some ID."

I look at Finnegan and he gestures we are ok.

"Oh ma'am, here's the thing. My buddy here did not bring his ID. Foolish of him, I know, but he just wanted to get out of the house and try out a club for the first time."

The teen just keeps flipping pages.

"NO ID, NO ENTRY." She was adamant.

* * *

"What are you reading? Is that '*Balanced*' magazine? I wish they would have more beautiful Black Locks in them like yourself. I could get lost in those black eyes for days.

"Truly, the world is missing out on how stunning Black girls are."

It felt so cheesy to hear, but to my surprise, she blushed. She smiled and looked at him with gratitude. Finnegan takes her hand and kisses it with charm. She almost sinks out of her seat.

"How long do you all stay open tonight?" he asks. She could barely respond,

"O—open to . . . 2 am."

"Ok, I'll be back around 11. Hopefully, you're still out here. What is your name again?"

"Elecktra," she responds.

"Aw a Lightening Lock, how sweet," he says.

I noticed her keychain definitely showed a golden coloration in the jewel section. She gathers herself and points her hand like a knife toward the club's entrance. We both walk in, with Finnegan looking more jubilant than me who looked baffled. "Alright Ashy, allow me to introduce you to your first club." He places his hands over my eyes as we walk through a small crowd and once he releases them, I am in awe.

Teens everywhere, walking around with different skin tones, different features and different EVERYTHING.

* * *

Asians, Blacks, Whites, Hispanics, it was a mixture of everyone. Again, I have to remind myself, these cultures no longer exist. It's all about their eyes, but even so, I see everyone.

Reds, Golds and Browns all talking.

The Black and the Violet girls were in a group on the side of the bar.

There are Blues and Greens having a drink-off competition.

It was everything you could imagine in a teen movie, except this was a club instead of someone's house party. "So teens can drink?" I asked loudly so Finnegan can hear me through the mixture of talking and music.

"Come now bro, you know the legal drinking age in all of Aether is sixteen. Just don't get too crazy with it and the cops won't try to kill you," he jokes.

He guides me to the bar, and we sit on top of two stools. Loud music drew my attention. Down one hall led to a dance floor and teens were all out there, showcasing their best moves. A slender, pale bartender greets us at the bar. Her height was about the same as mine and her skin was the color of my hair. Her eyes were the most lovely shade of light brown.

"Hey guys! What can I get you two to drink?" she asks. Her duty must be strenuous since she was the only person behind the bar. She carried a smile on her face the entire time.

"What would you like, Ashy?"

"I don't know. It's honestly my first time drinking anything other than holy wine?" I immediately start regretting I said that. He pauses and stares.

* * *

"Ma'am, how about two shots of rum and add a little spice?" he says. The bartender seemed delighted.

She pulls a bottle out and pours two shots into two small glasses. With her hand, she holds her fingers above one. "Unlock," she says. Some type of spice falls into the shot and she places it around the rim of the shot glass as well. She does this to the other shot and passes them to the us. "That'll be two tokens, please," she says.

Finnegan pulls two black tokens out and both have the number 1 on them. He hands them to her and turns to me. I was actually nervous at the sight of it. Finnegan picks his drink up.

"Cheers, bud!" he roars. I pick my shot glass up, nervously. I take mine slower than him. Finnegan took his like a champ, while I immediately start coughing.

"Ha, lightweight! Let's get a drink and take another shot. I promise it'll be easier the second time," Finnegan says. I almost fell out of my barstool. Finnegan request two more and the bartender makes them again.

"Ok, slow it down this time, buddy. Enjoy the liquor," he says to me. We say cheers again. I take the shot and this time I take it very slowly.

"Ok, now how was that, Ashe?" Finnegan asks. From my face you would've thought I had drunk acid, but I have to admit the truth. It was not that bad the second time.

"I didn't mind it." A slight hiccup comes out and we both laugh at the sound.

"Bartender, I think this boy is ready to graduate to a mixed drink. Gives us something nice that'll sneak up on you," he requests.

* * *

The bartender whips out several bottles and a plastic container of what looks like orange juice.

She swiftly mixes it all and sends the finished drinks our way.

Finnegan samples a taste of his and is delighted.

Because I was scared, I first sniffed the alcohol to assess its strength before I tasted it. It was fine. I take another sip and it was really nice. I think I can drink this and not feel sick to my stomach.

"You know this isn't too bad, Finnegan," I say. The atmosphere really dawned on me just how majestic it was. I have never felt this way before and as I look to Finnegan, I can't imagine what I could've done to meet such a genuine individual.

He doesn't even know about my Key.

"What you thinking about, Ashy?"

I immediately snap out of my own thoughts. "Oh nothing buddy!"

"You're an interesting character, Ashy. Why are you so guarded?"

I pause to think of an answer.

"You know, Finnegan, when you've been overlooked your whole life, it doesn't feel real when you finally get noticed."

"I get you, but life isn't about feeling ashamed of who you are. You can't help that you only have the Black, vestigial Key. Embrace it!"

* * *

"Wait, how did you know—" he cuts me off with a response,

"Dude please, I could see that jewel from a mile away. It's as black as that crow you feared when you first saw it land on that light pole."

I freeze up and stare at him. What else did he see? Did he witness . . . me making a shield?

"However, I must admit to being terrified when that Deadlock attacked you. To my surprise, it was gone when I opened my eyes. What did you do to make it go away?

"I mean, I'm not trying to be funny, but I know you Black Locks with all black HUEs can't manifest any active Key capabilities. How'd you make the Deadlock disappear?"

A sigh of relief came over me. He didn't see what happened, therefore is still in the dark about my Key. "Oh, I just yelled at it, man." We laugh, so I guess that means he fell for the lie. I take another sip and it was like time began to get slower and slower until it completely stopped.

I look around and now everyone is in slow-motion. What kind of sorcery is this? I look up at a tv hoisted above the bar and oddly it was like all the noise in the club went silent. All I could hear is the news lady on screen talk slowly, but audibly.

"Albedo and all the Warlocks are poised to make a new consideration on whether to reorganize a new government tomorrow, during council. Multiple restless nights last year from a protest group in the south district caught their attention.

"Evening Dawn Gold, a solid, led the group. The young lady made headlines when she left the Gold family's estate and joined Celeste Pollux's school of archeology and anthropology a couple of years ago. Albedo says that this will be the first time legislation from the south side will be considered because of her activism."

I gasp at the news revelation. "Eve said she was an activist."

Time starts to revert back to normal and I can no longer hear the news. "Ashe, are you ok?" Finnegan asks.

"Yes.. I'm fine, Finnegan. Hey Finnegan, can you keep a secret?"

Finnegan adjusts his bandana on his head. He looked more serious than before when answering. "Yes, I can keep one."

"What if I told you that I am not like those other Black Locks? What if I told you, my Key is not vestigial?"

I stare into his eyes. There's a slight tremble in them.

"I would have to see it to believe it, my friend. I can't believe anything I don't experience."

I take a quick look around and see everyone in the club all distracted by their own crowds. I raise my hand mid length and Finnegan takes notice. Black HUE starts to form around my palm and before it can fully encompass it, Finnegan grabs my wrist and lowers my hand.

The HUE disappears, and I looked up at a startled Finnegan.

His mouth dropped to the floor and his expression was as though he saw a ghost, or Deadlock I suppose for this world. "Ashe, you hav . . . an active . . .

BLACK KEY?" he asks, frightened.

"YES. Yes I do."

His face turns into a huge smile. "Dude, that's so cool!"

He turns to the crowd of people in the club's passing area. "Hey everyone, my buddy has an active Black Key!" He continues to state this in every direction. At one point, he even stepped on top of the bar and said it.

I reckon the noise was too loud for anyone to care. "Keep it down." I forcefully grab him by the arm and assist him back into his seat.

"Dude, I said, keep it secret. I'm not supposed to be showing off my Key to everyone."

He nods. "Ok, ok, Ashy."

Two girls walk in our direction, both brunettes. One could pass for White in my time and the other for Latina. Both were slender, sort of hourglass frames and wearing crop top shirts. I buck up the courage to sit erect in anticipation and, not shockingly, they looked past me for Finnegan.

"Who did you say has an active Black Key?" the one I thought was Latin asks. Her eyes were pink as cotton candy, while the other girl's eyes lime green.

"Why, my buddy Ashe here has an ACTIVE Black Key," Finnegan says. Both of the girls turn to me. They look less than impressed and then turn to each other to laugh.

"Stop lying! Black Locks always want to sell you a dream!" the lime-eyed Lock says.

* * *

"Newsflash guy, your Key used to be hot shit a millennium or two ago. Darwinism did you dirty sweety," the pink-eyed one says. They both giggle. My head lowers in shame. However, I attempt to find the courage to show them.

I raise my head and stretch out my hand. Focused, I channel black HUE to my fingertips.

Their necklaces bounce off of their chests as if my HUE were levitating them. They both stared in shock. After the HUE disperses, I lower my wrist and simply look at their scared expressions. "Ha! I told you," Finnegan says.

Both girls immediately turn to each other and pause before turning back to me.

I can feel the alcohol slowly taking over. I realized, "This is what being drunk must be like." Before I know it, both ladies are sitting on opposing sides of my lap. My shock forced me to play it cool to avoid weirding them out.

"You know, I always wanted to see what it was like to hook up with a Black Lock before I die. It's on my bucket list," says lime eyes, as she caresses my face with her hand.

"I dated a Black Lock, once. Something about those pitch black eyes just turns me into a Blue Lock, if you know what I mean," the pink-eyed one says, with a wink. It took me a second to realize what she was saying, but by the time I did, she was already kissing my cheek. The other girl kisses me on the mouth.

I didn't know what to do, so I just sat back and allowed it to happen.

"That's what I'm talking about, Ashe!" Finnegan cheers from the side. The girls get more and more frisky until a male on the side approaches.

* * *

"Ivy, what the hell are you doing?" he asks in a tough tone. The lime-eyed one turns with her lipstick disheveled and stained all over my face.

"Woody, wait! It's not what it looks like."

Woody, looking like a muscular lumberjack, was too tall for me to accurately describe his height. His skin was dark as burnt brass and hair was in an afro like mine. His eyes were green and piercing through me.

"Get up, Black Lock! I'm about to kick your ass," he says. I place my hands up in a servile manner, but before I could speak, he immediately throws a punch in my direction. He misses and hits the bar, leaving a noticeable dent in the wooden counter.

The girls run off in separate directions, while I struggle to stand up and dodge an array of fists. He swings again and again, with me barely escaping them.

"Ashe, fight back!" Finnegan calls.

That last punch misses and I point both of my hands in his face. "Concentrate," I tell myself. "UNLOCK." A black spherical shield surrounds me and propels the gargantuan male backwards. He demolishes parts of the bar after falling into it. The crowd finally pays attention, but questions spiral over what actually happened. The shield disappeared so fast, I hoped no one saw it. I look on, thinking the dude might be dead.

His eyes twitch and he slowly rise out of the wreckage.

"YOU BASTARD!" he yells. He charges at me once more. Finnegan grabs me and we turn around to run. On the way out, we pass a table of teens. Finnegan grabs a glass of water off their table and dips his hand in it.

* * *

It glows with the blue HUE. "Skiddy, unlock!" He throws the water from the glass on the ground. The giant male runs behind us and his foot touches the water. Immediately he slips. He tries to stand, but slips again. He tried again and continued to fail.

Outside, the girl with the magazine is now looking at herself in a small pocket mirror. She obsesses over her black eyes, as she had done since Finnegan complemented them. We run out the door and Finnegan makes it a point to address her.

"I'll be back for your number, beautiful!" he yells.

We run down the street for at least a mile. Further and further, we treck to a secure place.

After realizing we could no longer see the club, we slowed down. We stop to catch our breaths before looking at one another and laughing.

I look at Finnegan with importance. "You know, you're not half bad, Ashy," he says.

"Likewise. Thank you for the fun night, man." He stretches his left hand out to shake. I thought it odd, but I follow with my left hand. We lock hands and for a moment I felt this crazy world might not be all that bad.

"I hope to hangout with you again, Finnegan."

"I hope so too, Ashe."

Finnegan then unlatches my watch and snatches it off my wrist. He opened his flask with his right hand. "Skiddy, unlock!" He slings water out the flask. I immediately try to catch him but slip and fall.

"Finnegan, what are you doing?!" I lay defeated on the ground. Finnegan backflips far into the sky and onto the top of a small business building's roof.

"Remember what I said, Ashy. Life is about seizing your opportunity and living in the moment. Until next time, champ," he says. He jumps onto another building and then another.

I lay on the ground in my own remorse.

A tear falls from my eye. Before I can fully process it, steps approach me from the side. I look up and it's the cop from earlier, looking rather perturbed.

"It's time you pay, you little smut Lock," he says. I just lay my head on the ground and stare off into the starry sky.

Locked Inside

The clock on the wall said 6:01 am. I had sobered up significantly since last night's shenanigans. I clearly understood that my judgment had been poor and vowed to never drink again. Looking around, it's no wonder television always made jail look like a terrifying place.

Even in the year 4003, it's still not a place I'd ever wish to visit.

However, here I am.

This huge cell behind bars holds about forty of us. It held almost exclusively Black Locks (shocking). I stood in the corner, looking disheveled and tired.

I had not slept in the six or seven hours I had been in holding. All around were other Locksmiths who were yelling and screaming at each other. One Lock pointed his fingers at a boy and threatened to light his clothes on fire if he didn't give him his lunch.

The Lock complied and handed it over.

"This apple is rotten!" he says, while the other dude laughs.

* * *

"I guess it was a bad batch," the other male stated. He places his hand in his pocket to conceal the green HUE on his hands.

Several dudes were simply looking for a reason to be heard. Screaming nonsensical noise in the airwaves, but few were on the wall, in hiding, like me. It was obviously a juvenile detention center, and you didn't have to check anyone's ID to see it.

These kids were acting like animals in this containment. A mini food fight even broke out, to my dismay. I ducked a flying sandwich that stained the wall besides me. Mustard bled from the spot I was standing and touched all the way down to the ground.

I breathed, "This is trifling." I hoped no one heard me. One fellow catches everyone's attention and, surprisingly, all the fighting stops.

It was a morbidly obese fellow who walked to the center of the cell to relieve himself in a toilet. The smells of excretion filled the cell the moment he sat down. I felt appalled and slightly relieved that the fighting stopped. He was a pale fellow and kind of resembled a guy in my class back home. His eyes were black as mine. With everyone's attention on him, he began to talk.

"Listen up! Enjoy the fun, because those guards will be serious when they return. They are gonna strip you of your humanity and identity. They've already stripped you of your livelihood.

"Once you're in here, those judges don't give a shit about you. Hell, I'm not even talking about the Warlocks. YOU KNOW ALBEDO DON'T GIVE A SHIT.

"He watched you with his 'all-knowing mind' commit a crime and didn't stop you. I am talking about those lower end district judges. Those Black-eyed sellouts on the south side enjoy ensuring that we all remain in this shithole until we die."

The room oddly seems to agree as I notice several people nodding or replying "True" throughout the cell.

"They always say you can do better than this, but the truth of the matter is, Black Locks like us are designed to fail. Look at that guy's keychain," he says, with fingers pointed at me. I froze up being put on the spot like that. "His shit is pitch black. You know he won't have no opportunities in this world. Man, if any of you make it out of here, just keep your head up."

He flushes the toilet. The room seems to be in a more tranquil mood, oddly. Locks start to converse and make small talk amongst one another. All I can think about is how I'm going to get out of here.

Let alone, that hoodlum took my watch. It was the only thing my mom left me as a memento, other than my first name, on those steps. When my dad answered the door, he said all he saw was me in a small wicker with a watch and a name tag.

Learning that my mom clearly traveled through time to drop me off in the past, does kind of add a little spice to the story, I suppose. But all the more reason to be upset about the watch.

Nonetheless, my main focus is not being stranded here.

I didn't even know Madam Celeste's home number to call when given the opportunity to have my one phone call. I've simply accepted my fate. My stomach rumbles as I'm in deep thought.

It was making a terrible bubbling sound. "Whatever was in that drink is not sitting well in me."

Staring at the toilet, I walk over and just look at it. I'm afraid that if I don't relieve myself, I'll make a mess in my clothes. Using the stool in front of all those dudes makes me uncomfortable, however. I know I have no choice. A shivering tear falls from my eyes as I slowly pull down my pants.

"It's ok Ashe, it'll all be over soon," says a voice close to me.

I look around and I don't see anyone standing next to me. No one besides me or close enough for that noise to be that audible.

Who was that?

What was it?

I pause for a second, as now I assume I'm going crazy.

"Yeah, definitely not drinking anymore," I remind myself. In an instant, a cop comes to the cell.

"ALABASTER BLACK! Are you in here? Someone's here for your release."

I immediately pull my pants back up, even though they were never fully down past my hip. Not one bit did I care. I ran out of the cell and rushed out of the holding room. The cop barely had time to close the bars behind me.

I run, skip, and gallop to the front of the building, where I saw Celeste standing. A woman behind the desk was handing her paperwork as I arrived.

"His court date will be on the 8th," she tells Celeste. The guard opens the door and I run to give her a hug with an open embrace.

* * *

"Celeste!" Instead, she smacked me in the face with a folded paper.

"Ashe! Go outside and get in the carriage," she commands sternly.

I nod, "Yes, ma'am."

All the excitement had left my body. I walk into the brisk winds and noticeably stumble a bit before getting in the carriage. I guess the alcohol hasn't fully worn off.

Once inside the carriage, I see I am sitting next to the same man that took Celeste and me to Albedo's castle. He sits silently, shaking his head at me. A quick glare in my direction and then he looked forward for the rest of the duration. Celeste follows soon after and gets inside. She slams the door and immediately starts yelling before I can open my mouth.

"Ashe, how could you leave Jasper alone to go out with a stranger? Is there anything you want to say for yourself?"

I try to respond, "Celeste I apologize for—" but my sentence is completely cut off with her hitting me on the head with a rolled-up piece of paper.

She does this again and again. Thus, the entire ride home consisted of this, as the carriage flails through the early morning sky.

The sun was the brightest it had ever been on this winter day. The 3rd day of the Red month was circled on the calendar and I found it hard to believe I had truly been here for three days so far. After getting yelled at the entire ride, we finally made it home and I immediately crashed on the couch. By the time I woke up, it was almost midday already, and the sun was shining. I showered, puked and ate breakfast in that order. Celeste was in a more delicate mood during our first meal of the day, and she even smiled every so often while stirring her grits.

Even though I was knocked out on arrival, she delayed breakfast so we could all eat together. Noticeably, during breakfast, Eve didn't make eye contact with me once.

I don't think it stemmed from disappointment. She was just engrossed in reading and decorating a poster.

I thought it was odd of her to do this during breakfast, but immediately after serving everyone our portions, she was consumed with fixing up this poster. Don't think she even ate.

Back in the room, the clock struck 12 pm noon on the dot. I lay on the ground, doing push-ups with the help of Jasper. By help, meaning he sat with his legs crossed on my back.

Every time I lowered he'd say, "Say it."

I respond, "You were right, I was wrong." Then I would rise to repeat.

"Again!" he commands.

"YOU WERE RIGHT, I WAS WRONG."

This continued until like my 15th push up. He finally let off my back. He stretches out his hand for me to grab and helps me off the ground. "Never again, Jasper. I won't doubt your discernment."

* * *

We both laugh. I lay under the bunk bed and rest my head on a pillow. "I see that scar has healed up quick, Jasper. Do you still feel any pain?"

He responds, "Nope, that was some powerful HUE that Bluesmith had. He left no bruise and no scar."

I think for a second.

"Didn't you use that same combination for Eve?"

Jasper nods. "Yes, I did, and her ankle has healed up nicely."

I rise off the pillow and sit upright on the bed with my feet touching the floor. "So, it is possible for two different Locks of two different colors to use the same combination?"

"Well, partly. There are two combos that every Lock should master before they die: 'Unlocking the Craft' and 'Unlocking the Hippocratic,' respectfully as they are written in combo books. These two combinations are the only ones that can be assessed across the color line.

"Both do something different depending on the Key, but they seek to accomplish the same goal."

Healing abilities would have been useful in our situation.

"Are you excited about today? I think council is in an hour or so and it's your big day."

Jasper's words remind me. Today is the day I get nominated by Albedo and the other Warlocks to take his place. Maybe I should learn a couple of moves in case they question my authenticity.

* * *

"If you like, Ashe," Jasper happily says, "I can teach you those two combos."

I pause for a second, before responding, "I would love that, Jasper."

We both head out of the room and down the hall.

The sound of the news catches my attention and then I see Celeste sitting on the couch, cradled, looking worrisome.

"Madam Celeste, what's going on?"

She neglected responding to me because of how focused she was on the news.

"Jasper, you remember Kindle Mars? The Black Locksmith who used to be addicted to meteor ash? He is being given a trial date. They are accusing him of setting a man on fire in the middle of the street on New Year's Day."

Jasper gasps, "Wait Madam, are you talking about that old man who repeatedly went to jail for using meteor ash? When did he even get out to kill someone?"

Celeste shrugs her shoulders. "I don't know, sweetheart, but what I do know is there are a lot of witnesses that say they saw him specifically light this man on fire."

On the news, a woman with violet-colored eyes testifies to the camera.

"Yeah, I saw it happen right here. The old man used a forbidden combination and killed that other guy. That Black Lock killed that poor man and then tried to claim it was self-defense." The lady on the screen was talking in a very concerned tone. The news shows a picture of an old, dark-skinned man with a heavy beard.

The hair was black with grey strands and all his mugshot angles showed the same expression. He looked miserable and numb. Underneath the picture, the name was: Kindle Mars.

The news anchor reported, "He said he used the forbidden combination to protect his granddaughter from harm. He is pleading with Grandlock Albedo to spare him, since it was complete 'self-defense.' Now, the combination he used is a quaternary combo affectionately named 'Unlocking the Wildfire' in the red HUE books.

"Even in self-defense, only special Locks can use quaternary combos. Black Locks, in particular, are forbidden from even learning them. This will be a case to watch in the upcoming days."

The news shows what looks like a six-year-old on screen. This must be his granddaughter. Brown skin and hair texture like mine, my eyes grow gloomy for her future. Her beautiful black eyes impressed me, even though I fear the color. But I can't look at that beautiful little girl and think maleficence would come from her.

"That poor girl. He's been in and out of jail her whole life. Nothing is stable in her world," Celeste says.

The news makes it a point to show protesters who eagerly espouse the unfairness of the case.

"When a Black Lock defends themselves, we get treated like second-class citizens. They don't allow us the same basic human decency to preserve ourselves that every other Lock, from Red to Violet, is allowed. But it's only bad when Black Locks do it," a woman on tv complains, while looking at the screen. Eyes, black as mine, but her skin was pale, and she was fairly blonde.

"He is being held with a 1,000 tokens bail. The granddaughter is being cared for by her aunt on the south side, but the Mars family is begging for a change to the laws about who can and cannot use quaternary combinations," says the news lady.

I just stare appalled. Such a sad story.

"It was almost a parade on the south side when he got out of jail and beat his addiction. But now he's being separated from his family again," Jasper says and shakes his head.

"What exactly is meteor ash?" I looked around, confused.

"Made from meteor remnants and other substances, it's an illegal drug and the meteor remains are the main active ingredient. It's a powdery, black substance that addicts use like a hallucinogen.

"Authorities prohibit it, and users usually receive a three-year prison sentence plus fine," Celeste says.

"This man has been back and forth to jail for using that drug for almost 100 years. This unfortunately is not the first grandchild of his who he will leave unintended while he rots in prison. Then again, they may throw the death penalty at him," she finishes.

As sad as it all sounded, I realized Eve was missing. "Wait, where is Eve?"

"She's in the front with her activist friends. I'm supposed to be up there with her, but you asked me to teach you some basic combinations," Jasper answers.

* * *

I gasp, "I remember seeing a news special on her last night at the club. They said her and her activist friends are the reason Albedo is considering stepping down."

Celeste nods. "Absolutely, they are! That is why I was rushing you from the castle yesterday. I knew the moment he said you were being considered to take his spot, that it was Eve and her activists efforts that had truly paved that road. I didn't want you to accidentally say anything that might change his opinion." Celeste adds a pat on my back, cheerfully.

To be honest, I desired to hear Eve's activism in real time. I walk toward the front door. I know it's colder outside than it is warm, but I had to open the door, just a crack, to hear Eve.

Standing with her back facing me in the front yard and over two dozen youths in the crowded area, I see Eve with a black bandana on the top of her head.

It was tied to let her long brown hair pass straight through it. All the other members also had black bandanas in the crowd. Most were not even black-eyed, which meant, these were the Nonblacks that Jasper spoke about who were rallying.

As expected, Eve was curating a pleasant push for change. Her tiny but plump, pink lips pressed against the megaphone in her hands. With her right fist in the air, she screamed, "We need change today! When we show up to this council, we will make a change. We will be heard. AND finally, Grandlock Albedo will step down and let the south side choose a Warlock. This is something that hasn't been done in hundreds of years. Pat yourselves on the back, because all your protesting will make history TODAY.

"There is a saying that Madam Celeste taught me: 'THE BEHOLDER OF BLACK IS THE LAST TO MAKE IT TO THE FINISH LINE OF ITS

BEAUTY.' I used to really have to think about what that meant. Just look around. Black tokens, hip black jeans and hey even the Warlocks robes are black. We adorn the color everywhere unless it's in the eye of the beholder. We will stand up with our bandanas adorning the color black and stand together with those who can't just take the color off, TODAY."

Eve's crucial words reverberated through the yard and all the way down the street. I saw several neighbors throwing up their fists in support all down the block. Her crowd goes wild and every word I felt inside gives me goosebumps.

I close the door and have to pause. This girl is amazing. Someone like her, using her voice and privilege to help these Locks, deserves a Nobel Peace Prize. Ha, I wonder if they even still give those out. I turn around to the tugging of Jasper on my pants' pocket.

"Ashe, council is going to start soon. Do you still want to try to learn a couple of moves now or do you want to wait until after council?"

"I would like to now, little buddy." At my response, we both head to the backyard, through the kitchen and out the backdoor.

Outside, the backyard was rather spacious. There was a nice gate separating Madam Celeste's yard and the neighbors. It was picturesque. A burn pit, with diagonally placed logs forming a diamond shape around it, was at the center. The rest was a well-kept yard full of grass.

"We used to have a shed, but Madam Celeste let the hurricane blow it away so we could collect the insurance," he says.

The sound of something crashing against something else catches our attention. We look up and two Black Locks are battling each other on the roof of the house.

They both looked dirty with torn clothing. I think one was even wearing hand-me-downs. The one on the left channeled a lightning bolt from his hand and the other a fireball from his palm. The elements crash and explode, with neither being successful at harming the other. In between the two was a hat with a couple of tokens in it.

"The first person knocked out puts four tokens in the hat this time," one of the fellows said.

"HEY! Both you get off Madam Celeste's roof and go fight for money in an alley or somewhere," Jasper yells.

They both take notice and scurry away. One grabs the hat before they effortlessly jump to the neighboring house and then the next, and so on. Jasper sighs and looks at me. "Did you all have to worry about people fighting on your roofs back in your time?"

"No, I don't think most people could reach the roof when they jumped."

Jasper seemed baffled at my response. "Hmm . . . Humans really were like neanderthals," he says.

"Ok Ashe, let's get started, because I don't think we have much time." He pulls out a dark brown book entitled The HUE: Bistre. I look at its cover and try to remember where I heard that word used.

"Oh, your last name is Bistre." I recalled that fact, and he affirmed it with a nod.

"Yes, this is my family's combination book. You're always entitled to your family's book, even if you don't attend the House. I was adopted at a young age, so I got older and joined Celeste's House. Thus, I have two combination books: this one and this one." Jasper pulls out another book. This time a black book entitled, The HUE: Archeology.

"You'll soon learn that all the 'pseudo combination books,' as I call them, are usually black with no family name attached," he says. He hands me the black book, and I opened it.

The first page was a history of how Huemans came to be. "The meteor crashed and left the black ashes everywhere. People began to notice a change in themselves, Keys, HUEs, etc."

The following page discussed the HUE. According to the text, the Key is the soul's link to the natural world. The expression of said Key is the "HUE."

It lists the Keys in this orderly fashion: Red Key is Fire, Brown Key is Earth, Gold Key is Lightening, Green Key is Wood, Blue Key is Water, Violet Key is Wind & Black Key is (vestigial) Void.

The text talks about the complexities of the Keys and what each Key is said to control: Fire configures heat, conflagrations & temperatures and Earth controls mineral deposits, the crusts, sand, etc.

I take a more deep dive into the book and turn the pages until I see the first set of combinations. The 1st one on page 16 is titled "Unlocking the Craft."

"Found it!" I was elated to finally find a combination.

I read aloud, "Unlocking the Craft is one of two primary combinations that every Lock with an active Key should know. Depending on the Key, the craft created can be a beautiful illusion made of light by the Gold Key or even sounds of a musical symphony in air created by the Violet Key. That and all artistic expressions in between are what Unlocking the Craft sets out to create. For art is what you create, and all things created are art." The passage ends with numbers: 1, 3 & 3.

"The Craft is a primary combination that every active Locksmith should know. The other being Unlocking the Hippocratic, which is our ability to heal one another," Jasper says.

"Now there are four types of combinations:

1.) Primary combinations: These are the combinations that everyone, no matter the color or creed, should know and master. As described, it is just those two.

2.) Secondary combinations: These are combos that specialize in certain areas of Hueman activity. The bulk of your combination book should consist of secondaries.

3.) Tertiary combinations: These are combos that can take or give a life instantly. Every Lock should learn one tertiary combo before they die.

4.) Lastly, the quaternary combinations: These are combos that can drastically change the scope of the environment. They also can give or take a life. Case in point, Mr. Mars using Unlocking the Wildfire to kill that man, allegedly.

"We call quaternaries 'forbidden combos,' and only some people may even learn them. It is kinda unfair, but makes sense. We can't just have anyone using them, but a whole group of people being banned from learning them altogether, I think is unjust. I digress, however."

Jasper takes a deep breath and closes the book.

* * *

"That is why we wear these keychains, Ashe. When they are on, it stops you from using a combination past secondary. Removing it implies intent to kill."

A quick flashback comes over me and I remember all the various combos I've seen since I been here. The shield or dome thing I created. The flying balloon from Phoebe. The craft that Eve created and Jasper when he fixed my watch. Even that water combo that Finnegan used. It was easy to put those all in a couple of the categories that Jasper gave me.

Hmm, what would the craft look like for me? Could it create a new cosmos? But wouldn't that be a quaternary? I guess there's nothing to know if I don't try.

I position my hands out into the yard toward the burn pit and focus.

I close my eyes and dive deep into my body. Through the flesh, I see that black padlock again. The foggy HUE disappears and reveals my inner padlock.

I carefully twist it to 1, then 3 and then to 3. I open my eyes. "Craft, unlock!"

I exclaim and, to my surprise, to no avail. No HUE, nor craft was created.

I stare at my palms and try again. Same as before with my padlock: 1, 3 and 3. "Craft, unlock!"

Still nothing.

"I think my HUE is broken, Jasper."

"No, I think you just are not imagining your craft. You have to imagine the craft and send the HUE outward. It's written on that page."

* * *

A quick look again on the page and he was correct. It says indeed to focus on the craft and create by channeling HUE outward. I flail my hands as though I were removing something sticky and try to reposition them. "Ok, this time I will focus."

The sound of a chirping bird catches my attention.

It chirped as if in distress. I turned to the oak tree in the yard and saw it was a small robin limping with a crooked wing.

An older bird flew from the tree to assist it off the ground, but failed.

This must be a mom and child. The mom kept flying upward and then down to the ground as if to encourage the bird to fly too. But the bird would not fly. Its wing was severely damaged.

"This bird must've fallen from the tree. Well, Ashe, here is a chance to try another combination if you dare."

He flips the page in the book to a different combo.

"Unlocking the Hippocratic is a primary that is designed to heal a minor wound or fracture. The combo uses HUE to repair or reinstate a damaged body part back to its normalcy," the book reads. The page ends with the numbers: 9, 1 & 6.

"Well, I guess I can give it a try." I walk over to the bird and Jasper follows distantly in anticipation. I place my hands above the wing of the crying fowl and close my eyes once again. The padlock becomes visible and I turn the dial to 9, then 1, and lastly, all the way around back to 6.

* * *

"Hippocratic, unlock!"

HUE forms up around my hands. I feel it flowing toward my palms and then it disappears. "Damn! I almost had it."

I immediately ask God for forgiveness for swearing.

I say again, "Hippocratic, unlock!" The HUE comes and goes once more. The bird still chirps in distress. I take a moment to concentrate heavily on the wing.

A voice I had heard before, but couldn't identify, says to me clear as day, "Make sure you keep the same mood throughout. Your HUE is sensitive and you must maintain the same mood throughout the combo."

I flinch in fear. "Is everything ok, Ashe?" Jasper asks from behind me.

"Ah, yes, it is, Jasper," I lied.

What was that?

Who was that?

I look around, and no one is there. I lower my hands again hesitantly and try to apply that line of reasoning. "Ok, I'll keep the same mood throughout. Hippocratic, unlock!"

The HUE from my palms shoots to the fledgling, and I see the wing repair in real time. When the HUE disappears, the bird starts to fly upward toward the tree. It makes it to the end of a hanging branch and jumps its way back into the nest where the mother resides.

* * *

I stare at my palms with shaky eyes.

One triangle on my keychain spins and turns black. Jasper jumps with glee. "You did it! You did it!"

I take a moment to reassess. I definitely know I heard something talking to me. But where did it come from? "You're not hearing things, Ashe. It is me," the voice says again.

I freeze in my place.

"Is there someone there?" I asked softly, out of Jasper's earshot.

"Yes, I am here and I've been here since your youth. I'm your HUE, Ashe," the voice says.

I'm baffled and lost for words on how to even respond.

My HUE . . . is talking to me?

"Ashe, look!" Jasper says, with his fingers pointed toward the front of the house. A crowd of people march down the street. It felt almost like a marching band coming down the road.

"The council is about to start, we better hurry," he says. We both rush indoors through the back. I close the door and lock it but I'm not moving as quickly as Jasper, since I'm still in shock.

I wondered if I were to close my eyes if I would see this voice talking to me. But, no time. Celeste threw a coat on and headed toward the door. "Come, you two, we don't want to miss the council." She holds the door open for the two of us and we hurriedly walk through as she closes then locks the front door.

* * *

We join the crowd and pleasantly march with them. This was a crowded lot.

Shoulder length apart, there was no space to stretch my arms. I struggled to see Celeste and Jasper in the crowd. I could at least make out the top of their heads, so I knew they were close beside me. Ahead of the crowd, Eve and her crew chanted, "No justice, no peace!" on their microphones.

I trail behind the crowd down the street. People leave out their houses with children in both hands and join the crowd. More and more people come and join as we trek to the area to see the Warlocks.

I am getting bumped around left and right every time I stop walking, thus I have to keep a steady pace.

At some point, my mind goes into autopilot, and I close my eyes while walking. I take a deep dive into my body and try to find that voice again. Where are you? Don't go silent now.

Where are . . . HERE!

A dark room door shrouds my vision. The door was black with a white chain covering it. I touch the knob and it hardly twists. Surrounded in almost pitch black, in any other setting, I'd be terrified. However, I remember having this dream before. Since I was in elementary school, I have visited this exact same door, but I don't recall ever getting this close to it.

"Are you on the other side of this door?" I wait for a moment, but no response.

I put my ear to the door and hear something speak. "Yes Alabaster, I am here."

"How do you know my name?"

* * *

"I told you I've been here as long as you can remember. I've been locked inside you and I've been waiting for you to let me out," it responds.

The voice sounded like a grown man, so that made it even more mind-boggling. "If you are an extension of me, why don't you sound like me?" I wait for a response.

"I AM WHO YOU ARE DESTINED TO BE. I am not simply you, I am your HUE. I am you at your fullest potential. You should not shy away from me, because I am the only thing that will help you fight for the plight of the Black Locksmiths."

"Why are you just now exposing yourself? If you've been in here for so long, why is this our first interaction?"

"Ashe, Keys don't just show themselves at any given time. It takes time. I needed to get a good vibe of you. Now, I am certain you are the true savior of this time."

I pause and reflect.

"Savior? That's the same term Phoebe used, to refer to me."

"Phoebe was right to call you that. There is mischief and misfortune afoot coming up in this council, Ashe. As much as you can, make sure to always protect your HUE," the voice says.

"What are you saying?"

There was no response.

* * *

"Hello? Hello?" I heard nothing from the other side of the door.

I hear, "Hello? Hello?", echoing around me. I pan out of my interior and I come back to the tangible world.

Jasper is patting me, saying, "Hello? Hello?"

"Oh, my bad, Jasper. I was just in deep thought."

I look around and the crowd has made it to a section of town where there are no huge buildings or houses. It was just an open field with a stage, reminiscent of a concert from back home. Chairs decorated the massive area in a half circle around the center stage.

The chairs followed the color scheme: one black chair and then a white chair, so forth and so on.

Celeste, Jasper and I all sit together in a row. Looking forward, Eve and her protesters were front and center.

They stood, in fact, while hovering over their seats. They still chanted, "NO JUSTICE, NO PEACE!"

Grandlock Albedo appears from behind the curtains on stage. The crowd, including Celeste, goes wild at the sight of him approaching the center of seven podiums on stage.

The noise overshadowed the protest. I could see there were some Black Locks who hesitated to espouse the same level of happiness to see him.

Most sat and softly clapped, if at all. He extends his hands in a Christlike manner, and black HUE emits from both palms.

* * *

He claps them swiftly and stars with galaxy materials flail at everyone, but disappear.

It was a nice attention grabber. "Order everyone. We will now begin. Though you all know me, as I know you all, I want to formally reintroduce myself as Grandlock Albedo—the oldest Warlock in the world. It is here, in Medley, where the first Huemans manifested. So since the beginning, there has always been something special about Medley.

"Unprecedented times have brought your Warlocks together here today. We have maintained balance in this part of the world for centuries. We have kept Medley safe and orderly as the beacon of the world's justice since we took our positions.

"Come, let us greet all six of the other Warlocks together."

He turns his head and the crowd claps. Six men and women walk out from behind the curtains to a barrage of applause. They all dressed in the same black robe as Albedo. To be centuries old, they all maintain well posture and walked swiftly to their respective podiums.

The first being a man with my skin tone, but black hair with ashes of grey. I would associate his looks to that of a Middle Easterner back in my time. His eyes were as red as a stop sign.

The next was a tall dark-skinned Lock with an afro that went around in a perfect sphere. His height superseded all the other Locksmiths' on stage. His eyes were brown and I would've described him as Black, back in my day.

The next man stands at the podium in between him and Albedo. He looked White aesthetically and his hair was gray with a waviness to it. He turns his

140

golden eyes slightly to Eve, who did not share the same smile as he. Something about it felt forced. He turns back to the crowd and projects a wider smile from ear to ear. "That's Eve's ancestor, Thor Gold," Celeste whispers across Jasper to me.

The next, on the other side of Albedo, is a green-eyed woman with olive skin and a heavy pink flower in her hair. With her glossy, brown hair texture, I would have thought she was Mexican, back in my day.

Next to her, another female stood at her respective podium. She was very young-looking for her age. A chocolate skin toned woman with brown dreads down to her waist. Her body was in an hourglass shape and she struck me as being the most youthful looking one of the Warlocks. Her eyes were very blue.

Lastly, a woman whose eyes were violet and her skin very pale stepped to her podium. Her hair was pin straight and black. She aesthetically looked Asian to me, but I know only from seeing them, back in my time, on television. All seven Warlocks are officially on stage and I have to admit that the mood changed the moment they entered. I felt as though I should feel honored that these individuals would even consider the likes of me to take their position.

The crowd grows silent as Albedo speaks. "Now, as you all know, we all come from the north district—" Before he can finish, there is a section of the crowd that applauds obnoxiously at the words "north district."

"Settle down. As I was saying, the Warlocks are always considering the needs of the people. A balanced world dictated that we tried every government since the day of the first Huemans. This past time, we have tried the aristocratic governance. This involved six of the noble families being courted with the offering to be the head of the town. We are the judicial and executive branch. Historically, you all have been the legislative branch, making laws and rules for us to set forth.

* * *

"What happens here in Medley is the blueprint for the world, as we are the beacon. To maintain order, we allowed each district to submit their top choices for representation. In a competition you've all seen in reruns called 'Unlocking the Truth,' we battled it out, and the north district won. Medley was the only town involved and the only town allowed to establish such."

I whisper to Jasper, "Unlocking the Truth?"

He whispers back, "Yeah, I recorded it a long time ago. This was like a centuries' ago competition to determine which district would win representation. Needless to say, the north side won." I turn back to Albedo's speech.

"And yes, the rules have always been to only listen to the legislative branch that we represent. It was how the Locks before us had established it into the World Constitution. In recent times, however, there were issues that even I could not foresee." The speech is paused by surrounding laughter.

"Oh, stop it Grandlock!" a girl jokes.

He continues, "There have been issues of colorism and classism. Medley finds itself sliding backward into the time of humans. If Medley slides, so doth the world. So for the first time in centuries, including before I took office as head Warlock, we will take in legislation from a district that we do not represent and in real time will let you know our findings."

Albedo looks to Eve. "Eve, we have received the legislation from you and your coalition. These are our findings." Albedo turns back to read off a list.

"The first piece of legislative would put time limits on those in office. To sum it up, the suggestion being one century at most. The last legislative act establishes a permanent democracy, ensuring equal representation and voice for all districts. We have reviewed this Eve, and as Grandlock, I thought it would be important to hear you out. There are improvements that can be made to our governance.

"To the latter legislative, we have ruled in favor of keeping this governance intact.

"We do determine this on the basis that we would have to respect the forefathers' and foremothers' wishes to keep the governance to who won the Unlocking the Truth Tournament.

"I was the ultimate winner, and I decided the aristocratic governance works best. With that being said, that opened the discussion on whether we should open the UTT back up and allow for a new generation of young people to replace us. This would permit the potential change to our governance.

"This was a discussion amongst the Warlocks. We are getting old and this is a reasonable consideration.

"We have to disregard this legislative as well. We are here to remain as your Warlocks until further notice."

Albedo ends with a ruthless tone.

An uproar can be heard all across the field and Eve's coalition immediately begins screaming.

It was so much noise, it was inaudible to decipher what was being said. I did hear Celeste say, "My HUE, all hope is lost." Jasper, seeing Madam Celeste cry, begins to tear up as well. He attempts to console her.

* * *

I turn all around and see multitudes of people, mostly Black Locks, in tears and inconsolably crying. It brought profound grief to me seeing the little girl from the news crying hysterically. Something about that little girl being so young and being understanding of this issue stood out to me.

A woman tries to console her. "It's ok baby. Auntie is going to make it ok," she tells her.

I couldn't bare to keep listening.

I drop my head into my lap and cover my ears. "Ashe," something whispers. It was that voice again. I dive deep back into my interior.

I open my eyes and in front of me was that door again.

"Ashe," it called.

"What do you want now?"

"I have a solution to this. Let me out and I can tell you. This is the combination to let your HUE's full potential out: 1, 19, 20, 18, 15, 16, 18, 15, 10, 5, 3, & 20."

"HUH?" I struggle to recall all the numbers in order.

The voice pauses and is silent for a second.

"If that is too much, try this one: 19, 5, 1, & 12," it says.

What is the legitimacy of this?

If I release my HUE to its full potential, could that sway the Warlocks to reconsider? After a short pause, I've decided there is nothing left to lose.

I look at the white chain on the door and notice there is a padlock on it to keep the door shut.

I turn to each number in order: 19, 5, 1, & 12. The lock comes off and the chain falls.

The door opens and the darkness behind the door was darker than I had ever known.

"Now what?" The more that I wait for something to walk through the door, the more cautious I become. I can feel a little bit of my phobia kicking in, but I pull it together.

Nothing answers. It is complete silence.

I lean in to take a peek, and the voice reappears suddenly.

"Oh.. and Ashe.. this is not your HUE." Immediately, a gray-colored hand reaches out the door. I recoil in horror.

"Are you okay, Ashe?" Jasper asks my motionless body. "Ashe? Ashe?" he continues.

He sits me up and opens my eyelids to reveal that they're rolled back in my head. I let out a loud, thunderous screech in the midst of the uproar. Jasper and Celeste immediately jump out of their seats.

Jet black HUE exits my body through my mouth, ears, and nostrils. The HUE shoots out of me and Albedo takes notice.

* * *

"Ashe?" he mumbles. Eve turned to see me, and even she was speechless.

The HUE flails out of me onto the stage.

The Warlocks all look in disbelief as the darkness materializes into a body. It was a grey skinned man, that when fully risen, was the same height as Albedo.

I rise to identify this figure. "A Deadlock!"

He slowly raised and stared at Albedo.

He faced him face to face in his torn clothing. "Hey, 'Grandlock' Albedo," the man says, staring at a motionless Albedo.

The Deadlock's eyes were grey as a cloud and his hands were dripping in black HUE.

Larceny

He stood in the face of the Warlocks with his head cocked to the side and a vicious smile. None of the Warlocks had bulged since he entered the arena and all of them were visibly in fear.

"ALBEDO," the grey man says, "Why do you have this look on your face? You are all-knowing, aren't you?"

Albedo's face grows irate. "Enyracl . . . I WILL NOT ALLOW YOU TO HARM ANYONE HERE!" Albedo storms him with black HUE exiting from his palms. "Unlock!"

A star the size and width of a hula hoop starts to spin in his hand, which was noticeably absent of a keychain. He throws the star so fast the naked eye couldn't catch it. BUT, the man with grey skin catches it effortlessly in the blink of an eye.

He takes aim before flailing it back. *SLASH*—It pierces through the red-eyed Warlock's upper torso and takes off the right half of his body, nearly decapitating him.

His blood encompasses the stage as most Locks scream in horror.

* * *

The grey-skinned man points his hand in the brown-eyed Lock's face. "Unlock," he calls. The brown-eyed Warlock's neck shrouds in black HUE.

CRUSH—The noise from the Lock's throat collapsing is so loud and vivid, it sounded like a branch falling from a tree. He falls to the ground besides the Red Warlock's pool of blood. Interestingly, the grey-skinned man holds out his hand toward the bodies and closes his eyes.

He clinches his fist and opens it slowly. "Now, return to me. Unlock!" A ball of red HUE and a ball of brown HUE leave each of the departed Warlocks' respective bodies and enter his. He visibly seems strengthened by this.

Albedo's chagrin grows.

"Enyracl! Die!" Albedo sends a comet from the sky hurling at the one he called "Enyracl."

Enyracl again derails the attack and retaliates with a larger comet from the sky. Enyracl, however, aimed it at the gold-eyed Warlock, crashing and crushing him. The impact effortlessly splattered his body.

Eve's eyes widen at the sight.

Enyracl closes his eyes and, just like before, forces a ball of HUE from the most recently killed Warlock. The gold HUE ball goes into his chest and disappears. Enyracl looks even more powerful. He turns back to the remaining four Warlocks.

The green-eyed Warlock tries to summon roots from the ground to entrap Enyracl. Her hands glow in the shimmering green HUE.

* * *

"You have done enough!" she says. The roots wrapped around Enyracl, paralyzing him. He stares at the Warlock deep into her green eyes. She begins to shake uncontrollably. Deep in her tissue, Enyracl's HUE surrounds her heart and causes it to stop beating. Her lifeless body falls to the ground. Enyracl steps out of the roots and forces a ball of green HUE to expel from her body into his. He then turns to the blue-eyed Warlock, who quivers to the ground.

"No, please, don't kill me!" she cries. Enyracl walks slowly toward her.

"Whatever you want from me, just take it!" she begs. Enyracl pauses in front of her. The violet-eyed Warlock now intercepts and surrounds Enyracl with a vortex made of wind. It grows taller and taller to be the size of a tornado. The sight mystifies the crowd. The tornado had violet HUE poured into it.

The Warlock thinks she's trapped him until black HUE overpowers the violet HUE. As if time were freezing it in place, the tornado slows down. The wind explodes and Enyracl remained in the same place.

"Unlock!" he commands. Immediately, the Warlock with violet eyes is demolished by an onslaught of meteorites. They separate her body into pieces. Enyracl then consumes her violet HUE. He turns back to the terrified Warlock with blue eyes as she shields herself in the fetal position. Enyracl simply takes a ball of blue HUE from her body and spares her.

She opens her eyes in shock. Enyracl now turns to Albedo.

He remained still for much of this ordeal. "Does the embarrassment of being a fraud encourage you to surrender your life to me? I certainly wouldn't want you to continue living a lie at these poor Locks' expense," he says, taunting Albedo.

* * *

"Enyracl, if you are going to kill me, then do it. You've taken everything from these people. You've taken their Warlocks. You've taken justice and this will reverberate across the world. If there should be any shame placed, it should be on yourself," Albedo says. He raised his hands as if to surrender.

Enyracl was visibly unmoved by his statements. "Albedo, there isn't a criminal charged with larceny that could ever be your match. What you've stolen from me . . . what you've stolen from the hearts and minds of all these Black Locks —it is unforgivable!" Enyracl produces the spinning star once more and takes aim at Albedo.

"This is retribution," he says. He throws the star at Albedo.

"Unlock!"

I jump in front of Albedo and create a shield to protect him. The star smacks the shield and even dispels it, but the shield derails the star. It instead flies into the sky until it dissolves into black HUE. Albedo looks down at me in awe. "Ashe?"

The entire townsfolk who attended this event looked at me with the same expression.

"Ashe, you don't know what you're doing. Stay out of this," Enyracl insists.

"NO. I trusted you and you tricked me. You've caused unspeakable horrors to this town, you demon." The sternness in my voice was felt throughout the field. The black HUE spirals around my fists as I contemplate my next move.

"Ashe, if you sympathize with the hate and mistreatment that these inferior Locks push unto Black Huemanity, then you're no ally of ours. You're a sellout, which is more dangerous. Therefore, we must kill you too." Enyracl makes meteors start to fall above Albedo and I.

We both throw our hands in the air and create a shield. The combined shield we create is strong enough to withstand the barrage.

"Ashe, how did you summon him?" Albedo asks me. Both of us are in the center of the shield, shrouded in darkness. Meanwhile, the meteors smack the exterior of the shield in every direction.

Celeste and Jasper both grow worried, but ultimately know they can do nothing to stop this.

I turn to Albedo in response to his question. "Unintentionally, I freed him after he gave me a combination."

Albedo pauses to think. "What would happen if you repeat that combination backwards? I think it's worth a shot to reseal him. Just repeat the numbers backwards and say unlock."

Albedo's plan was worth the try, but what if it didn't work? Will I have to live with this monster inside me for the rest of my life? What if he gets out again anyways? I take a few deep breaths. I remember the numbers and try to concentrate on reciting them backwards.

"12, 1, 5, & 19." I move my padlock number by number.

Once I reach the last number I yelled, "UNLOCK!"

The shield disappears and so do the comets. Enyracl started to levitate against his will, with black HUE surrounding him. His expressions turn from a vindictive smile to a frantic gasp.

* * *

"NO! Ashe, you don't know what you are doing!" Enyracl screams, midair.

His body starts to convulse. Soon, the red HUE ball flies out of his mouth into the atmosphere and disappears. Soon the brown HUE, gold HUE and all the other HUEs follow suit. The blue HUE returns to the Warlock, however. The crowd of townspeople watch in astonishment as this whole ordeal takes place.

His body starts to disintegrate until it forms into a half a ball of black HUE. It returns inside my body and I watch it go into the depths of me, behind the black door. The padlock sealed the reattached white chain, as if it had never been opened.

The blue-eyed Warlock was on the ground with teary mascara covering her face. She crawled over to me and kissed my feet. In all the wreckage and the bloodbath that Enyracl brought, nothing surprised me more than the applause from the crowd. They stood for an ovation while I stood there on stage in shock myself.

Is this real?

I know I've asked myself this for days now, but truly, what is going on? Albedo places his hand on the back of my shoulder. He thanked me, saying, "Without you, order would be lost everywhere in the world." I could barely hear him over the applause, but I understood his message.

I look to my keychain and none of the triangles changed colors. Surely, I just learned a new combination.

Albedo takes notice. "The inverse of a combo doesn't count, Ashe. The keychain does not recognize that as unlocked," he states.

Now it makes sense.

* * *

"Ashe!" calls Eve. She runs on the stage and embraces me. It felt so nice, but unexpected. "I was so worried about you," she proclaims, with tears in her eyes. Celeste and Jasper soon follow. They embrace me as well.

Not too soon after, however, Celeste smacks me on the head with a balled up piece of paper. "You could've got yourself killed, boy! Stop doing stuff!" she commands.

I simply nod. "Yes, ma'am."

The blue-eyed Warlock stood up and immediately stiffened up her posture. The resounding sound of applause for me seemed to amaze her.

"Albedo, I cannot do this any longer. Find yourself a new Warlock," she says to Albedo. Exhaustion echoed in her departing footsteps. Albedo's mouth drops as he turns to the crowd to compose himself.

"SILENCE!" he ignites. His hands clap and force a star ridden miasma to unleash into the crowd. Locks everywhere silence slowly. My eyes remained shaken. "Now," Albedo starts up, "These are unprecedented times. The slaying of all but two of the Warlocks in Medley is a disaster that's indescribable. The entire world will morn once they realize this tragedy! You all applauding shall suffer once you come to a moment of reflection." Albedo takes a deep breath and calms himself.

"Tonight will be like no other night in recent times. As you may have not heard, Warlock Siren has just resigned her role, which means I am the last remaining Warlock. With that said, I will be making a harsh decision tonight and will have to address the world. At 7 o'clock pm tonight, you all should be watching Channel 7. I will be giving Medley an address on my decisions going forward. Every Locksmith in town has a television or knows someone who does. It is my command that you all tune in. I will give my decision tonight."

Several people in the crowd enrage in uproar, "You're supposed to be omniscient! How could you not foresee this from happening?" one person asks.

"You mean to tell us this all-knowing thing was a lie? What's stopping these southern district people from stealing from us now? Surely, they have the incentive, since 'all-knowing' Albedo is a farce," says another.

Several Black Locks took offense to the last statement and collectively return insults. "That monster should've killed the whole north side!" says one, as several agree. The insults turn into a back and forth.

"It's not prejudice if it's true! I saw that Deadlock shoot out of that Black Lock's mouth. He then returned back inside him. As far as I'm concerned, he's just as guilty," a north side Lock says.

"He also saved Albedo. The most precious Warlock that YOUR district chose eons ago. Why else would everyone be standing and giving him an ovation the way we were?" a south side Lock asks.

Albedo grows restless with the banter. "I SAID SILENCE."

Again, everyone quiets down to his directive. "All of you are to be present tonight to my formal address to this town and to all of Aether. Until then, return to your daily activities. But let's be clear, you'd be a fool to doubt my omniscience. I expect everyone here to be present tonight for my speech. If not, there will be severe consequences." Several Locks begin to walk away from the area.

* * *

Empty chairs become abundant as several Locks abandoned the set-up.

In the front, near the stage, remains Eve's protesting group. Albedo turns to Eve. "Eve, I want you to tell your fellow protesters to go home." Albedo's tone turns severely serious. Eve, though hesitant, turns to her fellow protesters who were beneath the stage.

"Ok everyone, you heard Grandlock Albedo. We will respect his rank and reconvene after his address tonight. Let the fight for equality continue, my fair warriors."

The Locks, by the dozens, disperse and throw their fists in the air one-by-one at me. I return the gesture indifferently, but the more I saw the fists risen to me, the more I became inspired.

Albedo puts his fingers to his mouth and whistles. Immediately, a carriage with lion balloons landed. The door opens and guards from yesterday appear from inside it. "All of you, get inside now." Albedo demands.

I looked a bit confused. "Grandlock, are we just going to leave this carnage out here?"

He turns swiftly to me. "I will have EMT come handle this scene. The longer we all wait, the more traumatic it becomes. GET IN THE CARRIAGE, ASHE."

I turn to the group and we flock to his directive: first Madam Celeste, then Jasper, then Eve and then myself. Albedo gets in and closes the door. He and his guards sit facing us, while he sits directly in front of me. The driver in the front lifts the carriage off the ground with HUE controlling the lion balloons. The lassos tied to them make it easy for the carriage to hover above the stage and take off into the sky. We fly swiftly across the midday air.

* * *

It was beautiful outside but I was too afraid to continue to peek out the window, with Grandlock sitting in front of me. His stare was one that felt incriminating, but it could have been that he was still processing it all. The carriage flies higher and higher above Medley, all the while the wind gales strongly against it.

About 15 minutes later, we arrived at Celeste's home.

Water boiling on the stove, we all sit in the kitchen in silence. That is, Madam Celeste, Jasper, Grandlock and I sat in the kitchen. Eve poured water in everyone's cups to make tea. Outside in the front, the two guards stood at the front door side-by-side in the cold with colder expressions. Albedo used a combination that poured red HUE into their clothing to keep them warm.

Back inside, we finally all sit at the table with Albedo in anticipation. I could not gauge Eve's reaction to losing an ancestor in front of her eyes, but certainly wasn't going to bring it up either.

She sat next to me and placed her hand on my back. I immediately tense up at her touch. She's so beautiful. It embarrasses me how much I think about her. Albedo sat across from me. Perpendicular to my side of the table, Jasper sat across from Celeste. Albedo stands up, somewhat dramatically. All eyes follow him as he strolls across the room to the blinds.

He glanced in the backyard and then closed them.

He then walks back to his seat and sits. "Ok, let's get straight to the point. Unlock!"

He claps his hands together and gold HUE surrounds the room to create a visible outer space aesthetic. It looked like we were floating in the dark pits of the universe while still at the table. We all awe at the sight of stars and planets surrounding the path as we pass them.

Jasper hesitates to try to touch one until he sees it go through my hand like a hologram, reminding him this is just a crafted combination. "That's kind of neat," he says. The scene changes to a couple of young teenage boys who sat on the floor of a home in front of a man with golden eyes.

"Is that my ancestor that was murdered today, Albedo?" Eve asks in a concerned tone.

"No, my dear, I am much older than he. This is his great-great-great-great-grandfather. He was my cousin. We both sit here in front of our grandfather as he tells us how we were destined to be great."

In front of our view, this elderly man with gold eyes speaks to young Albedo and his cousin. "You are both destined to be great. Both of you are of the loins of the Gold family's finest. Zeus, you have seven gold HUEs in your arsenal that make you an exceptional choice to be in this year's Unlocking the Truth Tournament.

"Albedo, you were born with the rare genetic mutation that gave you all seven HUEs. By law, you are required to attempt the UTT," he tells them both. They attentively nod and maintain eye contact with him thereafter.

"See, back in those times, we had the UTT every few years. This is similar to how you all's system of governing was back in the human era, Ashe," Albedo says. "Each time we had a new UTT successor, we literally had a different governing system."

I turn to Albedo. "What is this UTT like?"

* * *

He flails his hand with the gold HUE and the scene changes.

Now the scene shows a group of twenty-eight teens, seven per side, with differing eye colors, glaring at one another. The way they formed resembled a box, with seven literally on each side. The setting is a forest with the four groups all clenching their fists with their respective HUEs covering them. Each team had a Lock representing one of each Key. They each also had one skeleton.

I curiously notice young Zeus in the middle of one group with golden HUE on his fist and young Albedo standing at the end of the group with black HUE surrounding his balled fist.

"The UTT is a tournament style competition between each side of the town, respectively. Here, you see Zeus and I standing before the east, west & south districts' teams. We represented the north side." The scene changes to these Locksmiths battling it out in midair.

You see one Lock summon a lightning bolt from the sky, while another blocks with a wall made of ground mineral he had conjured. There was a Locksmith made a cloud follow another Lock with the rain pouring from it. The Lock visibly suffers third-degree burns from the temperature of the rain.

Albedo just slings the opposition left and right with his black HUE. No one is able to touch him. I take a good look and gasp.

"Is that Enyracl?"

Albedo nods. "Yes, it is. At this time, the south district referred to him by 'Savior' prior to voting him into the UTT to represent them. We were among the last to have active Black Keys after the mutation occurred, which caused everyone else's to be vestigial."

* * *

Enyracl is the same height and complexion as Albedo. Both even share the signature skeleton eye color—grey.

"Albedo, you disgraceful Lock from the north side. You dare to look down on all of us Black Locks on the south side district. You will never be Warlock in this town if I have something to say about it!" Enyracl says.

"Enyracl, you are an embarrassment to your own kind. Black Locks deserve a leader who does not have a chip on his shoulder about what class he was born into." Albedo retorts.

All eyes fall on present day Albedo.

"I apologize if this is out of place for me to say Grandlock, sir, but that was kind of harsh," says Jasper meekly.

"This was a different time, young Lock. I think I deserve some grace for evolving in the last 7-8 hundreds of years," he explains. Celeste seemingly agrees, but Eve, Jasper and I struggle to show the same enthusiasm.

"He mentioned that he was a Black Lock, but his eyes are grey. Having grey eyes means he would be a skeleton, right?"

"Yes, that is correct. His parents were Black," Albedo responds to me.

"Remember Ashe, being a skeleton is a mutation, so Black Locksmiths can produce one as well," Celeste states. Now it made sense.

Back in the field, Enyracl has meteors fall from the sky unto Albedo, who destroys them with a barrage of meteors of his own.

* * *

The two stand at a stalemate. Enyracl breathes fire and aims it at Albedo. He vanquishes it with a wave of water.

Albedo, then switches his HUE from blue to brown and crushes Enyracl with two brick walls that slam and sandwich him in.

He looks to see if he is victorious and instantly, Enyracl makes roots and flora grow in such a way that the walls explode and a variety of plants surround him, unscathed. Enyracl harnesses a bolt of lightning in his hands and throws it at Albedo, who then creates a twister to the size of one of the tall pine trees to derail the lightning.

The twister approaches Enyracl, who then turns the twister into a sandstorm and sends it back to Albedo. Albedo produces a huge black shield, reminiscent of the one I would create, and disperses the sand vortex.

"Notice how neither is even yelling UNLOCK. That's how you know their power is on a different level," Celeste whispers. She was thoroughly engaged in the battle, as was I.

All the HUE disperses and then the two run at each other, fists first. They engage in a brawl where Albedo had the upper hand with a few face shots, then Enyracl kicks him in the rib.

Albedo hits a tree and Enyracl slams lightning into it. Albedo barely escapes and then he disappears. He vanishes into thin air. Enyracl looks around, but Albedo appears behind him and forces him into the nearby collection of trees. He holds him with the black HUE pinning his hands. The sounds of a huge siren going off, signalled to stop fighting.

Someone loudly proclaimed, "North district wins week five."

* * *

I turn to Albedo. "Who shouted that? The entire forest could've heard that."

Albedo responds, "That would be the point, Ashe. That voice was the voice of the previous Grandlock. Each week, only one side can be the winner and that involves teamwork. But I will speak about that at a different time. Let me show you the crux of this viewing, because I wanted you to know exactly how Enyracl came to be empowered and how he came to be locked away in you."

The scene shifts to Albedo and his six teammates being crowned Medley's new Warlocks. These people suspiciously looked nothing like the ones who were slaughtered today.

"Wait, so you were the last remaining Warlock of that group of seven that you competed with?"

"Absolutely, Ashe. The ones who stood by me today were descended from these core six." The scene shifts to Albedo and his team. They were all clothed in the black wardrobe and they posed in a stadium in front of many cameras. People in the stadium cheered. The stadium itself had to house nothing short of 70,000 people.

"As I swear in as your new Grandlock, I will run this aristocracy with grace and with might," Albedo says.

The scene shifts to the seven Warlocks sitting around a globe, just like the portrait in Albedo's lair. "We ruled for an extended amount of time. Making sure all the needs of the town were being met. I felt secure in my leadership skills as head Warlock."

Celeste looked, and a warm smile appeared on her face. "This is so nostalgic, Albedo. I feel the memories coming back. I had forgotten a lot about my childhood, unfortunately."

The images switch to the Warlocks speaking, while present day Albedo narrates.

"Immediately when we took office, and the entire world switched to the aristocratic governance, we made it our mission to stop crimes and hold all misbehaving Locksmiths accountable. Our number one target was Enyracl. He had learned a forbidden combination that allowed him to steal others' Keys. 'Unlocking the Larceny,' as it was named. For obvious reasons, the combination was forbidden, and Enyracl included it in a combination book he authored, along with other forbidden combinations. We finally caught and jailed him. He was set for trial, but he soon broke free. We placed him at the top of the fugitive list the moment that he escaped."

The screen shifts to Enyracl being in jail and then to him using some combination to blow up the jail, just to escape by jumping out of the roof.

"I tracked him down through the forest and planned to kill him with a tertiary combination you saw him use today. The heart stopping combination that only requires you to look into your victim's eyes."

The scene shifts to Enyracl running through the rain in the forest with a black hood on. He jumps into the trees and jumps from branch to branch. He lands back on the ground and almost turns around, but stops himself before he succumbs to that temptation. "You will not catch me staring you in the eyes, Albedo," he says.

After running and jumping two miles, he slows down.

He catches his breath briefly and looks around in the ominous quiet.

He looks to see no one in sight. His mood calms. A quick glimpse into a puddle changes it all. Albedo's reflection in the puddle pierces through Enyracl enough to cause his eyes to constrict.

Enyracl puts his hand on his chest and clenches it. HUE surrounds his heart and causes it to stop. Enyracl falls face first into the wet floor. "WOAH! So you killed him and saved everyone, Albedo?" Jasper asks.

"That is not the end of the story. Enyracl easily became a Deadlock. Becoming a Deadlock drives most insane, but your life's combinations endure. He retained all the forbidden ones, including the Larceny combination.

"He eventually found a coalition of Deadlocks and taught them the forbidden Larceny combo.

"They began to run amok and by the hundreds. Medley was pillaged by these monsters, which under normal circumstances, wouldn't be able to run into people's faces and steal their Keys. This is where the rumor of Deadlocks stealing Keys originally comes from, by the way. Enyracl had created an army of them and taught them all the forbidden combination."

The scene shifts to grey-skinned maniacs running around taking Keys and leaving people lifeless. When all their Keys get taken, they collapse and their eyes turn grey, which I thought was weird. Both Enyracl and Albedo have grey eyes, yet they possess all the Keys. Visibly, I notice Celeste is becoming somewhat triggered.

Her eyes widen and she tenses up. I remember she said she was feeling nostalgia. Does this bring back sad memories?

"When all of your Keys are taken, you become a shell of a Hueman," she says.

"All seven of us Warlocks made an executive emergency ordinance for all the

Huemans in town to stay in the home. We also made it so that nothing could leave town or enter it." The scene shifts to a wildfire burning deliberately around town. A huge wall made of clay surrounding the outskirts of town. Wind and lightning are perilously active in the sky. To finish, a huge black dome-like shield prevented the entering or exiting of everything in town.

"Now, Warlocks attack!" young Albedo commands. All the Warlocks begin to demolish every Deadlock in the town. Albedo and his band of Warlocks meticulously destroy every single grey-skinned being. The Warlocks eventually left the town wrecked, but the monsters were gone.

The scene shifts to all the Warlocks surrounding Enyracl with their hands pointed out in his direction. "We finally catch this cretin and all the Warlocks were steadfast in their motion. He was in the middle of the town where today would be located exactly where the stage is," Albedo says. The scene shows what was the remainder of the town's people standing in every direction, waiting on the next move by the Warlocks.

Celeste gasps, "I remember this!" she exclaims. "I was a little girl in this field. It is all coming back to me now."

Young Albedo talks, "Now you meet the all mighty HUE, you piece of shit! Unlock!" Albedo's hand immediately slashes black HUE at Enyracl and balls of HUE flail from his body.

"You learned the forbidden technique as well, Grandlock," Eve assesses.

"I did, but only to thwart Enyracl. After this, I hid his book deep in my confines and no one has ever been able to view it," he says. Eve looked as though she believed him.

Enyracl looks visibly disheveled.

* * *

His body looked wrecked and torn. I look a little closer. He is holding something, however I am unsure what it is. It looked like a rag doll at first, but it was, in fact, a baby. A baby with white hair and a tag on his hand with a name on it.

"I will return one day and kill all of you. And if you are all dead, I will kill your kids and your kids' kids into the last generation," Enyracl says. The baby he held was half naked in a wicker basket. His hands glow as he raises the baby in the air. He claps his hands together, and the baby is gone.

The entire crowd, which includes a young Celeste, watched in shock. Albedo runs up and slashes the final HUE from him and it flings into the air. It was half a ball of black HUE. Enyracl disintegrates into ashes. The crowd is stunned, but not nearly as much as I.

I dropped my jaw and it remained there since I saw the baby with white hair. Eve clenches my shoulder to comfort me, as does Jasper. Celeste breathes a sigh of relief. "That's why I recognized you immediately," she says.

Albedo chimes in, "After the trauma of such a chaotic chain of events, it became imperative to wipe everyone's memory away as soon as possible with therapists who used combinations that help people to forget. Celeste, you are one of very few individuals who even is still alive from that time period."

Albedo turns to me. "So Ashe, your context clues are correct. You were, in fact, that baby. When only half of the black HUE came out of the battle, I got suspicious. However, finding his book of forbidden combinations explained everything.

"Several combinations were torn from the pages. However, I could still read a description of one, 'Unlocking the Confinement.' The user traps himself inside another Hueman, but has no autonomy to control their body. He is still capable of invading your thoughts and witnessing everything visible to you. He obviously used this combo to partially encase himself inside you.

"A piece of Enyracl, secretly placed inside you, awaited the maturation of your Key to use you to orchestrate his grand return. He couldn't just travel back in time himself, because he had been weakened and there was no guarantee he would have had enough HUE to return on his own. Ashe, this is why he needs you. You have seven active HUEs and he feeds off your energy.

"The stronger you become, the stronger he becomes. It is imperative that you never listen to him. When you were in the past and he was vanquished, I had full omniscience. The world was orderly because of fear of my all-seeing eyes. Your return, with Enyracl, has been the reason why I have lost all omniscience. But, I can tell you one thing. Since your return, I have searched nonstop for a combination to permanently eliminate him without releasing him back into the world. So be patient with me."

Albedo ends the combination and the gold HUE flails.

"Albedo . . ." I started up, "Why didn't you tell me about Enyracl when we first met?"

"Ashe, when you originally came, I lost omniscience instantly, so I knew something was wrong. Storm saw Enyracl's HUE chained behind a door inside you, but you didn't give any reason to suggest he had been interacting with you. I thought perhaps your body absorbed him and he became vestigial. Instead, he was still laying dormant.

"I began to think the power of your HUEs had taken away my all-knowing eye. Worse case scenario, I thought we were safe for at least one more day, or at least until I spoke to the other Warlocks on what to do about this matter."

***

Albedo looks downward in shame, before he gazes into Eve's eyes. "Eve, I argued hard to make a change in favor of your cause, but the other Warlocks outvoted me. In our discussion, we also talked about what to do with Ashe. Your ancestor, my distant relative, voted to kill him in order to rid the world of Enyracl."

Everyone in the room gasps.

"But, I argued in favor of your life, Ashe. I told them that it was not your fault a Deadlock was locked inside you. Killing you for a crime you did not commit would be unjust and disrupt balance, I told them. Thus, the plan was to bring you onto the stage and make you a Warlock. That way, you could be studied and watched over by me, until I found a combination to completely irradicate Enyracl. But as we see, that did not happen. If I could go back, I would've held you overnight at my castle. Now, I trust that you will not release him again—RIGHT?"

I hesitate, before nodding "YES."

Albedo stares at me with sorrow in his eyes. "Ashe, if I could use the Larceny combination to place him in my body and remove all this inner turmoil from you, I would. But I tried that when we shook hands, to no avail. He is stuck inside you for the time being. That grants you vast responsibility to keep him chained up."

My eyes veer off into the distance. I certainly know I CAN keep him chained up, but I don't trust myself enough to say I will. So far, since I have been here, it has been screw up after screw up.

"Ashe, I must be going. Thank you Madam Celeste, for all the hospitality. I have a very difficult decision to make about the future of Medley. By now,

Locks have already phoned their loved ones around the world about the chaos. Remember to turn on the television at 7 pm tonight, you all."

Albedo ends and hugs everyone before heading to the door. Before he walks out officially, he turns to me.

"Remember Ashe, Enyracl is no friend of yours. He will say anything to be released again. Only way he can have power is if you give it to him. Do not allow him to manipulate you into letting him loose. You don't deserve to live with the shame of bloodshed on your hands. Fool you once, shame on him, but fool you twice, then you're to blame."

I nod, numbly. The door slams behind him. I sit on the couch and collapse into my lap. The others stare from afar as though I had the plague. I couldn't blame them, because even I was clutching my chest.

"This monster, he is inside me, potentially forever. What if Albedo doesn't find a combination to dispel this horrendous bandit?" I begin to panic and talk aloud to myself. Eve, without hesitation, comes and comforts me. Her warm embrace was literally everything I needed at this moment.

"Ashe, while he has a checkered past, we must trust Grandlock Albedo will do the right thing. He promised you he would find this combination and I believe in him," she says.

"Eve, this feels so unfair. I should be comforting you. You lost an ancestor today because of a creature that I let loose."

Eve smiles at me before replying, "Ashe, that ancestor was no genuine hero in my life. While no one deserves to lose their life as he and the other Warlocks did, I try to look at the positives in situations. He did not support any of my group's causes and I think I can speak for many south district Locks when I say, the world will be better without him. As painful as it is for me to admit. I stand with and for the greater good of society." Celeste nods, as does Jasper.

With that, the rest of the night went rather quiet. All of us sort of stood around in our own spaces awaiting 7 o'clock to hit.

At the strike of 7, all of us gathered in front of the tv to anxiously await the verdict regarding Medley's future. Celeste had told about fifteen of her friends in other neighboring towns over the phone about what happened, so I can only imagine how this tragedy had spread like wildfire. We piled on the couch, with Jasper sandwiched in between Eve and me, while Celeste grabs the remote.

Eve had baked cookies, and they sat on a stand in front of us. Celeste finally turns on the television and didn't have to search hard to find the channel.

Apparently, ALL the channels were playing Albedo's address.

The scene shows a seat similar to the one back in the Oval Office from my time, but I can tell this is inside of Albedo's castle. With urgency, we await the fate of the once great town.

"We will now introduce, Grandlock Albedo," says a voice not identifiable on screen. Albedo finally arrives. He sits staring at the screen, hands clasped, dressed the same. He looked unnerved as he began his speech.

"Hello citizens of Medley. As you all know, today was a tragedy at its absolute finest. I know this turn of events has spiraled into a continuum of questions and that, at this point, the entire land of Aether knows. So to those who are watching this broadcast in towns around the world, greetings to you as well."

* * *

Little did Albedo know, he was correct. The entire world was tuning in to his address.

"I am going to be brief and to the point. What happened today resulted from an evil, malignant spirit that has refused to rest. A Deadlock named Enyracl who has continued to cause suffering to all those he has come in contact with. He was killed by myself and thought to be extinguished eons ago, back when I first became a Warlock. He comes from a time like myself, thus he has an active Black Key like myself. Now, with that, his presence stifled my Key from being used at its fullest potential, which is why I had a temporary loss of omniscience. He was using a combination to cause me to be unable to see the future. That ability has since returned. I can see with an all-knowing eye once more."

I looked at Eve, and she looked at me. "He just told a lie, didn't he?" Jasper asks.

Celeste answers him, "Yes, dear. But for the protection for all the Locks, it is best to believe that an all-knowing eye is watching."

Albedo continues, "Now, something else many of you witnessed today was a young man who came on stage to save me from Enyracl. His name is Alabaster Black. Somehow, he has traveled from the past to the present day.

"He is the last remaining member of the original family who had the Black Key. He is the only other person left on this planet, besides me, who has an active Black Key. He is sixteen years old and is a Black Lock on the south side of Medley. Far too long has there been a division amongst the differing sides. I will take my blame for not pushing for the agenda of all and only for some. So this has pained me in a way that has resulted in this drastic decision I am making.

* * *

"I am stepping down as Grandlock at the end of this year and giving a new crop of young people an opportunity to come step in to be the new Warlocks of Medley.

"What this means is, I am reinstating the UTT—the Unlocking the Truth Tournament. It is a necessity for there to still be order, so we must continue to select the best from our districts. However, this now allows for Black Locks to join the stage and potentially become Warlocks. Far too long have they been ignored, and that disrespect is partly the reason for the results today.

"Tomorrow, the entire town of Medley will get papers in the mail to vote on who you want from your district to represent you and your needs. On the 5th, we will reconvene at the same location as today to officially announce the UTT participants.

"BE WARNED. Medley is the beacon of the world. Who you choose will effectively determine the governance in every town outside of Medley as well. So pick accordingly. With that, I bid you all a great evening and may the HUE be with you." Albedo ends his long-winded speech and I stare in angst.

If the UTT returns, would the south side pick me knowing there is a monster still inside me?

A New Council

I am dreaming once again. I always can tell when I'm in a dream state. This window is in front of me like the time before, and there's that tree on the other side. I can't help but stare out this window. It's as though I can't turn my head to look in any other direction. To my horror, a bloody, grey palm smacks the window.

I open my eyes, and I was at the kitchen table. With clasped hands, like in prayer, I was unnervingly stared at by Eve and Jasper. "Ashe, did you fall asleep during prayer again?" Jasper asks.

"Yeah, I think I did."

"Ashe, you really have to get some sleep. I mean, you were up all night. You need to be well rested for your big day today," Eve says in a concerned tone.

In terms of a "big day," she is clearly referring to the council that is about to be held soon.

Sunday, the 5th day of the Red month—it had been two days since Albedo addressed the land of Aether. Yesterday, Albedo sent dozens of his representatives across Medley to collect votes for a special ballad.

* * *

KNOCK, KNOCK—"Hello ma'am, I am with the Albedo administration's travel team. We've been assigned to deliver a list of south district teens to every household. It is mandatory that everyone that is eligible living on the south side, vote for your representatives in this UTT. Once voting is completed, I will return these papers to your districts council and they will take it from there. May I please have your cooperation?" This message comes from a person dressed entirely in black, resembling a hotel bellhop, down to his hat.

Every house down the street from Celeste's had one knocking on each door, reciting some version of the same thing.

Every teen in town, including the jailed ones, were on the ballad, but each district could only vote for the ones in theirs'.

When one knocked on Celeste's door, she made sure EVERYONE voted for my name and my name only.

The representative made it very clear to the south siders that my name came with a cost.

Because of the controversy surrounding my role in the Warlocks' demise, and being from the past, in order for me to participate in the UTT, everyone on the south side would have to vote for me. This is why Madam Celeste was on their heels about voting. IT WAS IMPARATIVE.

Jasper and Eve were on the ballad as well, but they were asked to forgo voting for themselves in exchange to secure my spot.

I didn't have an ID, so I couldn't vote.

* * *

Now, I just sit at the table with my face in my hands and just shake my head.

Someone left the television on and I suppose it was some parade going on earlier today. A marching band group of young ladies, dressed somewhat scantily, were among my main focus points on the television. One young lady in particular had a long white glove on one side, up to her elbow, and a long black glove on the other side, up to her elbow.

Her shimmery one piece suit was skintight from the bra area to her crotch and she has knee-high boots to match it. She led the front of the parade, with all the other dancers and musicians behind her, following her command.

She was a brown-skinned girl, with her hair dreaded and slightly darker than her skin while her eyes were black. She had red HUE spilling from her hands. Sparkling flames shoot into the air and spin around, before popping like fireworks. It was such a spectacular display.

I turn back to Eve and yawn. She was right.

I was indeed tired.

Truth of the matter, I wasn't missing sleep haphazardly. Every time I nodded off, that demon was finding his way in my dreams. He keeps popping up in random moments, like when I dreamed I was walking on the moon. This fiend shows up riding a meteor past me, grinning menacingly.

"It's just hard with this demon inside me."

Eve looked so upset to hear that. "All the more reason why you must be a part of the UTT. Maybe in the course, you'll have access to combinations that even Albedo cannot conquer. Who knows, you might find one to silence Enyracl once and for all before Grandlock Albedo," she says encouragingly.

* * *

I turn to the stew she cooked for us and take a generous bite. The circled date on the calendar was Red 5th, 4,003. This was a very important day. Soon, we will know if I got the votes or not.

It was actually nerve wrecking. It's almost noon and I haven't seen Celeste all day. She came in real late last night and left real early this morning.

"Celeste missed dinner, breakfast and now lunch. Whatever the new council has her doing, must be serious."

"I think today they are counting the votes. As soon as they are done in each district, a siren is supposed to ring. That will signal for everyone to head to the middle of town," Eve says. In Celeste's absence, she really has stepped up to make sure we stuck to the kitchen schedule. She even assigned chores, like washing dishes.

"Yeah, and who knows how long that could take? They are counting thousands of votes on the south side," Jasper says. He attempts to slurp the residual broth from his bowl, but stops himself when he realizes the sounds were loud. "Bad manners," he deemed it. He then attempted to slurp silently.

I start to think, maybe it will take them a few hours. That could work out for me, because then I can take a nap. I slowly dose off and slowly fall to the table. My face landing in the boil of stew.

RING—goes the siren at a loud, high pitch.

I immediately rise from the stew and wipe my face with a paper towel. Eve and Jasper both look surprised by the sudden ringing. I wipe the final bit of stew from my hair and make eye contact with Eve. "It's time," she says.

* * *

Coats on, we walk out the door collectively. Jasper closes the door and locks it. All three of us head into a storming crowd on the streets. The whole town was headed in the same direction.

Not a person in the windows, nor were there any carriages in the sky. Everyone was footing it to the center of the town to hear these results. I ignored my queasy stomach, attributing it to falling asleep in my stew as opposed to eating it.

"Walking on an empty stomach isn't smart," a Black teen girl says to me. "I can hear your stomach growling from here," she says jovially.

"I know, right? It's crazy, isn't it?" We both laugh.

"I just want you to know, me and all my friends voted for you."

I turn to the girl with genuine gratitude.

"Thank you and your friends for your support." She nods and after a few steps, she disappears into the crowd. I barely staid in pace with Eve and Jasper.

When we finally approach the center of the town, all the chairs are organized as they were before. The stage and the field looked untouched and unspoiled. It was a far distinction from the tragedy two days ago at this very spot.

Only differences this time were the tall signs directing people where to sit. North side in the front and us south siders were to sit in the back. The east and west Locks were arranged to sit in the middle. Jasper, Eve and I sit in the back with the hundreds if not thousands of other south siders.

The front, closest to the stage, was a more polished group of individuals with colored eyes. They were all high-fiving one another and talking loudly and obnoxiously. The whole south side section in the back was silent. It was a sea of black eyes, silently awaiting the ceremony to start. I look over and see Celeste next to other personnel that looked to be in her age bracket or close to it. It was too many to count, but she makes eye contact with me and gently nods. I tried to get an insight from her gesture whether or not I got the numbers, but she simply turns to the stage. Albedo approaches the podium and all slowly silence.

All around the area were cameras attached to inflated animal balloons. You can see dozens of Violet Locks with HUE coming from their palms controlling the balloons.

They all had "Medley News" written on their hats.

The chilly breeze brought the only remaining sound as Albedo pauses for a minute at the podium.

"Good afternoon, to all of Medley and to all the world watching. I stand proudly here to induct the new candidates for the UTT. As you all are keenly aware of by this point, a great injustice took place here two days ago. Five of our seven Warlocks were slaughtered by an unsightly Deadlock named Enyracl. He came and attacked the framework of our governance and was successfully defeated."

That final sentence saw Albedo look out into the crowd. If I didn't know any better, I would've said he was making eye contact with me.

Albedo continues, "Here in Medley, we pride ourselves on being the beacon of the world. What we do will affect the world all over. Thus, I say with humility, empathy, and courage, that I will be stepping down as Grandlock at the end of this year.

* * *

"My vacancy will open the position for another person to fill. This individual will choose how this fine town will be governed, as well as who may or may not govern next to this new individual. To make this fair, as per past tradition, the only way to decide the next set of Warlocks is by reviving the UTT. The Unlocking the Truth Tournament is a controlled warfare that allows seven hopefuls from each district to interact and engage one another in a battle of power distribution. This competition determines which district's legislation will be considered.

"The Warlock acts as the judicial and executive branch, while each district is the legislative.

"The balance of power has always been as such and is established in the World Constitution to remain.

"Whatever happens here in Medley sets the course for what will happen around the world. I emphasize that as I turn the attention over to each district's council. Now, we will commence the reading of the names. North side, you are first."

Albedo directs all attention to a group of men and women of all shades dressed in very formal business attire. One such person catches Eve's attention. "Dad?" she asks in an astonished tone. An olive toned skin and silk wavy hair like Eve, he looked like he was very important. He was dressed very pristine. He makes slight eye contact with her before turning back to the rest of his council members.

A dark-skinned man with a neat haircut takes the mic from one of Albedo's aides in the crowd. This man's eyes are a few shades lighter than Jasper, but I could tell they were brown.

"We of the north side council have completed the voter count and these are our findings. The first individual we would like to nominate into the UTT with 20,005 votes is FENIX RED," the man says. The crowd uproars with cheer.

A young man that I would've pegged for Middle Eastern back in my time steps up on the stage. A dark tan highlighted his moderately muscular build. His serious, red eyes slice through the crowd as he stood on stage confidently with his chest out. His black spiky hair was partly in the design of a mohawk, but I felt it was too short to truly be that hairstyle.

Even from my distance, I could see his keychain had several red triangles, meaning this guy knows a lot of combos and is definitely one to keep an eye on. Fenix turns to Albedo, who has one of his aides give him a red book. Albedo gestures for Fenix to raise his right hand and he follows. He directs him to place his other hand on the book.

"Fenix Red, of the Red family here in Medley and direct descendent of my former colleague. You have seven red HUEs and are seventeen years of age. You are eligible for the Red Lock's spot in the UTT. Do you solemnly swear on the HUE book that belonged to your ancestor, to take on the rules and job descriptions that come along with being a Warlock?" Albedo asks.

"Yes sir, I swear," Fenix says sternly, without a stutter.

"I solemnly grant you the position of your district's investment. Everyone give it up for Fenix."

The crowd goes wild over Fenix. The north district council can be seen pleasantly enamored with this choice. Fenix goes and stands in the north section of the stage that has "red" written beneath his feet. The north district speaker continues, "The next name that I will call with 13,201 votes is AMBER BROWN."

* * *

179

The crowd goes wild and Eve's mouth drops. I turn to her, confused. "Wait, what's the problem?"

"Amber Brown is a model. She's graced the cover of '*Balance*,' the same magazine that Celeste did back in her time," she says.

Amber, who is a tall, statuesque young lady, walks toward the stage. As if being almost taller than me wasn't attention grabbing enough, she had the most ostentatious display of jewelry blanketing her head to toe. Pearls in her long brown wavy hair and two large golden necklaces dawned her. She had red ruby stones around her right eye making a design and blue sapphire stones doing the same on the opposite eye.

Diamonds covered her dress and her ears had shoulder length spiral crystals coming from them both.

Facially, she was literally everything Celeste described as balanced features: olive tone skin, brown wavy hair, the nose, the eyes that were not too far apart or close, lips that were not to luscious or thin, oval face and hourglass body that was not super thin, but had a subtle curve to it.

She walked on stage and spread her hands in the air to revel in the applause. I turn to Eve.

"Hey, isn't this a fighting competition?"

"Don't underestimate her just because she dresses nice, Ashe. She is just used to putting on a show," Eve responds.

Albedo now holds in his hand a combination book that is brown. Amber repeats the same gestures that Fenix did. She places one hand in the air and the other on the book.

* * *

"Amber Brown, of the Brown family right here in Medley, and a descendant of my former colleague. You have seven brown HUEs and are sixteen years of age. You are eligible to take the Brown Lock's spot in the UTT. Do you solemnly swear on the HUE book of your ancestor to take on the rules and job descriptions that come with being a Warlock?" Albedo asks.

Amber takes the mic and turns to the crowd.

"I just have to say thank you all who voted for believing in me. Thank you, daddy for announcing my votes. I had no idea that so many of you wanted to see me represent as a Warlock. I will make sure to not let any of you down." She gives the mic back to Albedo.

He looked unimpressed, while the north district screams in excitement.

"I do swear to abide by these rules and expectations," she says. Albedo nods.

"I, therefore, grant you permission to represent your district for this position," Albedo finishes and the crowd ignites in applause. The north side was truly the only group clapping loudly. The rest of the districts just clapped at a regular, uninspiring sound.

The man with the list sheds a tear. "That's my girl. NOW, next on the list with 18,331 votes is MATTE HARVEST."

The crowd gives a standing ovation before the boy even stands. He indulged in it with a smug smile. Eve visibly was appalled. I assume this is another person she is familiar with.

Her face looked like she was beyond repulsed, and I reckon her father standing in an ovation for this guy didn't make it better. The boy walks on the stage with his brown curls bouncing and making all the young ladies close to the stage drool over him. His skin looked like a suntan versus something more natural and he was a little taller than me. He was thin, with long limbs like a basketball player. His eyes were an interesting shade of gold that was darker than Eve's.

He gets to Albedo and places one hand up while the other on the golden book.

"Matte Harvest, of Medley's Harvest Gold family. You are seventeen years old and have six gold HUEs. Do you accept the rigor and the responsibility that comes along with being a Warlock? Do you swear to abide by the rules and the expectations?"

Matte answers Albedo, and I could swear he looked right in Eve's direction while doing so. "I do with my full heart, Grandlock."

"Well then, Matte, you are officially granted permission to represent and vie for this position in the UTT."

The crowd continues to clap and applaud. Eve looked unyielding in her disgust. I did not clap, nor did the majority of the south side Huemans.

"Next, with 17,413 votes, we call to the stage, HEATHER EMERALD," the north side announcer says. Many applaud, but I noticed a subtle pause beforehand.

I wonder, what's that about? Wait, Emerald? That's the same name as that old man with the store on the south side. The produce man has a child on the north side?!

I look through the crowd to find him and I finally spot him after having to turn around in my seat. He clapped subtly, but I could see the burden in his eyes. I know that expression all too well. He was conflicted.

"Any story on how this guy's daughter ended up on the north side and he lives out here with us?" My curiosity spiraled for an answer.

"Well first, it's his great-great to infinity great granddaughter and second, she and her twin brother lost their whole family to an infection that only affected them," Jasper responds. "I don't remember the ins and outs of it because I was so young when it happened. But I think only a few survived and for whatever reason, her parents put her twin out of the Emerald household. They raised her on the north side, and Mr. Emerald raised her twin," he says.

"Who is the twin?"

"No one has seen him in years. He basically disappeared without a trace, but I hear he sends postcards to Mr. Emerald every so often. BUT WHO KNOWS?" Jasper finishes.

The girl, Heather, was a curly redhead with pale skin and freckles. Compared to other girls, she wasn't particularly tall or short, but her creepy smile was undeniable. I could tell from the way she smirked on stage that something was off.

Yet, the north side was going wild in obnoxious praise.

She turns to Albedo and stares unflinchingly at his grey eyes. Silence comes over them as neither relents on staring. "Place your hand here and raise your other hand as such," Albedo commands and shows her. Heather slowly follows suit.

"I do," she says. Some in the crowd laugh.

* * *

"It is mandatory I address you and then ask the question, Heather. Heather Emerald, sixteen years old from Medley's Emerald family. You have six green HUEs. Do you solemnly swear on this green book, from my departed colleague, to abide by the rules and requirements of you as a Warlock?"

"I do," she responds, coldly.

The crowd goes wild, and she dawns that awful smirk once again. Albedo points her to go stand beside Matte in her "green" circle.

All four of the north side picks stand side by side.

The announcer calls the next name. "With 13,102 votes, the next name we call to the stage is ARK NAVY."

The crowd oddly reacts with a resounding gripe.

"Oh my goodness, people voted for that guy?" one person asks.

"Well, no one in the Blue family lives on the north side, so we had to settle on the Navy family," another person responds.

"His family are well-known plumbers, but people on the north side know them for their unprofessionalism and laziness," a woman stated.

The north side announcer looks around and is baffled. "I said, ARK NAVY!" Still no one answered. "Ark, where are you?" he asks, sounding upset. Someone nudges a snoring male in the crowd. He wore a sort of blue sari, and an elongated mallet rested between his legs.

He awakens to the fifth or sixth nudge.

* * *

"Huh? Where am I?" he questioned.

"They are calling you on stage. You are supposed to be representing us in the UTT," the girl who nudges him says. He immediately jumps up. "You guys chose me? Get the hell out of here!" he says as he prances onto the stage.

He was about five 5 feet 9 inches and of medium build. In my time period, his physical features would have labelled him East Asian. His hair was straight and brown, in a bowl-cut.

He stood next to Albedo, basking in the cheers and jeers with an unbothered smile on his face. With his mallet raised in one hand and his other hand on the blue combination book, he looked Albedo in the eye as he repeated the same requirements. "Ark Navy of the Navy family, you are eighteen years of age and possess six blue HUEs with one black HUE."

The north side visibly looked displeased at that final revelation about his HUE. Albedo didn't care. He asked him if he would abide by the rules and then asks, "Do you accept this offer?"

Ark smiles and looks crafty with his navy blue eyes. "Now Albedo, someone as all-knowing as yourself doesn't need my answer. I will play along, though. I do not decline this offer," he jokes.

Albedo looked unimpressed, but many throughout the crowd giggled.

"Yes, Grandlock, I accept," he says, correcting his tone.

"I am granting you permission to represent the north side," Albedo says and points Ark to his section, next to Heather.

The announcer shakes his head as though annoyed.

* * *

"You do not make jokes with the Grandlock," he says this under his breath, before continuing his list, "The north side council will now call to the stage, with 16,000 votes, JAY VIOLET."

The crowd claps and cheers, but more humbly for Jay than they did for the people before. Jay too resembled the Asians I saw on tv back in my time and even had black hair. It was cut in a more emo hairstyle, however.

Jay gave off this androgynous look, but I could tell from the walk this was definitely a female. Standing at a height of 5 feet at most, Jay was short and slender.

She placed a hand on the violet book.

"Jay Violet, of the Violet family here in Medley. You have seven violet HUEs. You are fifteen and your ancestor was gruesomely murdered two days ago. Now, you have the opportunity to take her spot, young lady."

She nods at Albedo's words with a soft smile.

I noticed on her back was an instrument with a yarn textured covering that contained it.

She carried it using a fabric strap. She stood in front of the towering Grandlock calmly. "Do you accept the rules and creed of a Warlock?" Albedo asks.

Jay remained silent.

Albedo turns his head, but maintaining eye contact. He looked like he was waiting for her answer, as was the crowd.

* * *

"Well, Jay?" asks the announcer in the crowd on the mic. A raven flows downward and lands on her shoulder.

"YES I DO," it says loud and resoundingly in a young girl's voice. It creeped me out, but the crowd goes wild.

"I suppose that was a combination," I whisper to Eve.

"Yes, Unlocking the Craft, but Wind Key style. Sound is just a manipulation of air, so Violet Locks are the masters of ventriloquism. Only the powerful ones can make animals speak for them, though," she replies. I take note of that.

"I grant you permission to vie for Warlock," Albedo says to her bright smiling face.

Jay goes and stands with the other Locks. All six of them are supposedly the best the north side had to offer, yet I can't find one of them remotely likeable. I don't know if it's the general smug that the north side carries or if my intuition is taking over, but all of these picks cause me to feel disconcerted.

The announcer looks at his list and takes a couple of minutes to look at something. "There is one more who will complete this six and make it a seven Lock collaboration. This individual will complete our representatives and will save the north side from bowing down to the rest's legislation. This individual is ROAN GREY."

The crowd again gives a standing ovation. It was so thunderous that my chair shook a little at the sound. A dark-skinned male with a muscular build walks up on the stage. He was not obnoxiously buff, but you can tell he worked out.

* * *

He was probably my height or taller and his eyes were as grey as Enyracl's and Albedo's, the latter standing in front of him.

The most stand out feature to me, however, was his dreads. They were back length dreads. Most were black, but there were speckles of pure white dreads all throughout his head.

I had never met someone around my age with white hair like me.

"Wait, he's a skeleton? Like Albedo?!"

Jaspers confirms, "Correct. The World Constitution dictates their upliftment, so a vote for his competition entry was unnecessary."

I remember Celeste saying this same thing to me in so many words.

Jasper speaks once more, "And one more thing, I forgot to tell you Ashe, skeletons are sterile. That is why you don't see a long line of Albedos running around. If that were the case, I'm sure he'd have chosen a monarchy system of governance."

Does this mean his Black Key is active too? Naw! Albedo said he and I are the only living Huemans with the Black Key.

Would he lie about that, like he is lying about his omniscience?

"Roan Grey, sixteen years old and a skeleton. Our constitution dictates your path, and sir, you cannot opt out of this competition. But do not see that as a hindrance, for all the world is designed for your leadership to flourish. Please take your place next to Jay," Albedo says.

Roan walks silently to his group and all seven stand in unison for the first

188

time.

Albedo pauses briefly and stares at the crowd of well over tens of thousands of Medley residents. He turns his attention specifically to those in the front, the north siders.

"Get a look at your new representatives, north side!" he says and all clap in an uproar. I notice that many of the Black Locks on the south side don't share this enthusiasm. Even the west and east kept clapping, but it completely ceased on the south side.

Albedo turns to the south side.

"Now, it is your turn south side council. It is your turn to call out your list of representatives. BEFORE we start, a quick prelude to this vote. As you all know, there is an individual from a different time period who randomly showed up. This individual has an active Black Key like myself. He harbored, unbeknownst to him, a bloodthirsty Deadlock named, Enyracl, inside of him." As he speaks, the north, east and west immediately start booing.

"SILENCE," he commands. "As I was saying, I cannot ignore that this young man, in his ignorance, released Enyracl into the world, but with his benevolence, he also sealed him back up.

"This young man is tortured as we speak, with a demon living inside him.

"So with that comes a lot of dissonant thinking. On one hand, he is a powerful Lock with seven black HUEs, more than me, I add, but he is also partly responsible for the great injustice that took place."

Eve places her hand on my shoulder after he made that last claim, because she could tell that upset me.

* * *

"So with that, Alabaster Black, please stand up," Albedo commands.

Rising slowly from my seat, the colorful eyes on the north side startled me. I looked to Celeste for comfort, but found none.

"I have introduced a special request that made this dilemma fair for all. Alabaster was allowed to be on the south side district's ballad." Immediate outrage takes place on the north side.

"However, only if he receives every single eligible inhabitants' votes, can he win the south side's representation," he says, immediately silencing all complaints.

I can tell from the sounds and gestures of the north that their tone had changed up to a more hopeful one.

"Now, south district council . . . read your findings," Albedo says. I turn to the south council and almost catch whiplash on how quick I spun to see their results. The crowd grows silent, with all the Black Locks on the south side nervously awaiting. Celeste stands and in her hand was a list.

The aides pass the mic to her.

"This is the south district's findings. Of the 24,002 eligible Locks who voted, Ashe, I mean, ALABASTER BLACK, received 24,001 votes," she says.

You could hear a pen drop, briefly.

The north side engulfs in cheers, while the south side moans and groans. The Black Locks start to weep and get rowdy.

* * *

"WE CAN NEVER DO ANYTHING RIGHT! I HATE BEING BLACK!" one says.

"I SHOULD'VE NEVER TRUSTED NONE OF YOU HEATHENS TO DO THE RIGHT THING! CAN'T EVEN VOTE IN YOUR BEST INTERESTS," another Hueman can be heard saying.

Celeste calls out, "SILENCE." Everyone quiets down.

Now all eyes are back on her.

"The reason why there was one short vote is that one eligible voter is no longer an inhabitant of the south side, or the town, for that matter. If I am correct Grandlock Albedo, the conditions of the vote were for every inhabitant of Medley to be counted. If one wished to leave town, they would not have faced the mandatory elective process.

"Thus, as it stands, ALABASTER RECEIVED ALL THE VOTES ON THE SOUTH SIDE DISTRICT."

Celeste finishes her reading, and all eyes flail to Albedo for his response. He blinks a few times and then that last blink was long.

He opens his eyes. "Yes, you are correct, Celeste. Therefore, we fairly elect Alabaster to be the south side's representative."

The atrocity that Black Locks felt immediately did a 180 in real time. Those same Locks bashing one another, immediately hug and some kiss.

"I love being Black!" the tune changes to. Jasper and Eve both hug me profusely. They were in shock as they push me to walk toward the stage.

* * *

I was so stuck on being chosen that now it didn't feel real. Celeste smiles and claps while holding backs tears, (unsuccessfully).

The whole thing turned into a parade of sort.

A group of Black Locks grab me and hoist me on their shoulders to carry me to the stage.

Upon reaching the stage, I hop off the shoulders. I walk toward Albedo, past all the blank faces of the north side district, pass all the sneers of their chosen representatives and pass all those bawling their eyes on the north that were so confident the south side had been checkmated.

I stood before Albedo and he tells everyone I'm sixteen with seven ACTIVE black HUEs.

Noticeably, there was no black book. Albedo didn't have an expression worth noting on his face, but I would say it was somewhat indifferent.

With my right hand raised, Albedo asks me the question I've been rehearsing my response to since Fenix got chosen. "Alabaster Black, do you accept all the rules and commit to perform all the duties required of a Warlock?"

My eyes shake before I take a deep breath. I respond, "I—"

Ashe's Choice

"Sometimes it's scary when you have the trigger in your hand and you have to pull it." I remember this quote from my father when we went hunting years ago. I don't think I was any older than five or six. Slowly, my memories are returning in this lawless world, and I thank God for that.

When the memory fades, I am looking Albedo in the face as he awaits my answer. There was a translator on the stage for the deaf who was at a pause, awaiting my decision.

"If God-willing, I will fulfill these duties. I accept," I say. The crowd goes insane.

Fire erupted from the fingers of Locks in the south district, popping like fireworks.

There were Locks throwing balls of lightning to one another like a football. This almost turned into the parade I watched on television today. I stand still before being directed to go stand in my district's section.

Respectfully, there was a circle labeled "black" that I stood on. I turned my attention to Celeste and the council. "Wait, if I got all the votes, then how are we choosing the other six?" I murmur.

Albedo began, "We have a unique situation requiring sensitive and respectful handling. The rule was for all the south district's votes to go to Alabaster in order for him to participate in the UTT. That rule was met, but that leaves no votes left for the other six representatives. With that in mind, I find it to be fair and balanced to allow Alabaster to choose the other six.

"You were met with unusual circumstances and you overcame them. It's only fair to allow you your own personal choice of those individuals who will fight next to you and represent your district. To be fair is to be balanced. This will be your choice and your choice alone, Alabaster."

Albedo stuns me. I think I can hear a slight hesitation in the cheers from the south side now. Of course I can imagine why. Some guy pops up in town four days ago and now is given the power to make such a pivotal decision. An aide directs me to come back to the podium. Grandlock Albedo politely moves aside to give my hesitant feet some room to step up.

Staring into the crowd, I nearly faint.

I finally find the courage to speak after a deep sigh and a quick prayer.

"First, I would like to say that I prefer to go by Ashe." I gauge the crowd's reaction and it was mute. "Second, are there any of you who feel comfortable representing the southern district?" Many eyes showed curiosity, yet nobody approached the stage. I turn to the section and see that we need someone to fill the "red," the "brown," the "gold," the "green," the "blue" & the "violet."

"Is there anyone?" glancing at the crowd, I asked again. I gulp as the nerves set in.

* * *

I can feel myself getting noxious.

A little girl on a balloon flies from the crowd.

I knew her outline before she got close enough to be identified. She jumps off her horse balloon and approaches the stage.

"I WILL STAND NEXT TO YOU, SAVIOR!" Phoebe says. She touches down on stage and stood in front of me, groping my leg into an embrace. Her scary, black horse balloon, "Pegasus," was floating nearby, causing me a slight tremble.

"Phoebe, are you sure you are ready for this? It will involve a lot of dedication."

"I AM," she says with a youthful glow. Her lack of worry spoke to her innocence as I stepped aside to allow Albedo to grab the violet book. She places her hand on it with a smile that could brighten up the sky.

"Phoebe Saturn, thirteen years of age and descendant of the Saturn family lineage. You have two violet HUEs and two black HUEs. This makes you eligible to take on the rigor and responsibility of the Violet Warlock's position. Do you swear to abide by the rules of being a Warlock?" Albedo asks stoically.

"I do, Granddaddy Lock Albedo." She cheerfully clasps her hands down by her midsection. She places her hand back on the book, awaiting his reaction.

"I grant you permission for the position. Give it up for Phoebe, everyone."

The crowd goes wild. Phoebe goes and stands in the "violet" section for our district on stage. Albedo moves to the side again for me to address the crowd once more.

"Now, that's one. Is there another?"

The crowd looks around, again. One girl raises her hand stiffly in the air. She stands with confidence and walks with grace toward the stage. I get a good glimpse of her and recognize her face. It was that girl from the parade I watched earlier. That confident young lady that led the marching band, shooting fireworks from her fingertips.

She had mid-chocolate skin, free of blemishes, and dark brown dreadlocks. She had typical balanced features, but her face was more round, with a tiny nose and tiny cheeks. Although her luscious lips didn't match her skin tone, they harmonized with her hair. Her striking black eyes gave away her heritage.

Her height and body type, I would say, mirrored Eve's as she carefully walked to the stage without a change in her pace. The closer she got, the more I realized a pink ribbon was in her hair, tying her wavy brown dreads in a ponytail. She comes on stage and I greet her with a handshake. It was firm and very formal on her end. Takes me a moment to realize this is the same girl I spoke to this morning that said she and her friends voted for me.

"My name is Ashley Aries. From the south side, I am fifteen and part of the Aries family. I have three red HUEs and four black HUEs. I would be honored to represent my district and help restore order to it," she said decisively, impressing me. I turn to the crowd.

"Do you all want to see Ashley stand with me?" I changed my tone in an attempt to hype up the crowd. I get a joyful response, so I step aside and let Albedo approach her with his colleague's book.

"You stated everything for me, Ashley. We will not waste time rehashing that.

Do you swear to abide by the rules of being a Warlock?" he asks.

"I do solemnly swear, Grandlock Albedo," she says passionately, and the crowd goes wild. Ashley goes to the "red" section and stands there while a smiling Phoebe greets her with a wave. She returns that wave and all the attention is back on me at the podium.

Looking around, I find Eve. I stare at her as I knew she looked back at me. I want to call her name, but I can see a slight hesitation in her eyes. However, I could not imagine her passing up a chance of social justice.

I started to say her name, but the sound of another voice interrupted me. A male, all the way in the back, stood as far from the stage as was visible.

"Wait! I wish to cast my vote," he says.

I almost have to squint to see this dude walk all the way from the back to the front.

He walks steadfastly as everyone turns to see who he is. Jasper's eyes widen. "Wait.. it can't be . . ."

Eve gasps once she recognizes him. Other south side individuals start to take notice of who this young man is and I'm still left trying to figure it out. Celeste's mouth drops and she turns to Mr. Emerald. His eyes look as though they were filling with tears.

He makes it to the stage and begins to walk up the stairs. He pauses mid stair to catch his breath and stares at one of the north district Locks on stage. From all the expressions I could see, the only one who reacted to his glare was Heather, the Lock vying for the Green Warlock's position. The boy had mid-length curly blonde hair sitting on his head like a mushroom. His skin had been very tanned, and he had a large bag on his back like he had been hitchhiking.

If I am 5 feet 10 inches, this guy has to be about 5 feet 8 inches, but his upper body was very muscular. His greenish colored eyes look all but warm and inviting.

He stands in front of Albedo and lifts his hand. Between two of his fingers was a note.

"I got this in the mail. After moving next door to Blend, I wanted to return for Medley's special Warlock election. I share dual relations with both towns, so I rushed home. Is it too late to vote?" the boy asks.

Albedo was very calm with his answer. "Yes, it is. Votes for the south district have already been tallied."

I draw an air of curiosity. "Who would you have voted for?"

He responds swiftly to me, "FOR MYSELF. I wish to join the UTT."

I was a bit shocked, but I didn't know if I should be relieved. He does have green colored eyes and we have an empty green space behind me.

"Alabaster Black, or 'Ashe' as he likes to be known as, won a special election where all the south siders voted for him. Due to this, he and solely he, is to determine who will stand next to him in the UTT. He is the only other member on this planet with an active Black Key," Albedo says.

The boy looks at me with an insulting expression as though I was scum, then changed it up readily. He approaches me and stood about a foot in front of me.

* * *

"So the rumors are true? My name is Heath Emerald," he says, trying to shake my hand.

He had the biggest and fakest smile on his face. At least that's what my intuition saw. But I couldn't process that before looking into his name. "Emerald?" Is this the guy Eve and Jasper spoke about? This would mean that girl . . . Heather is his sister.

I turn to look at her, and her menacing smile turned into a scowl like no other.

I shake his hand, though it felt untrustworthy.

"Would you grant me the ability to be in the UTT? I promise to perform all my duties," he promises.

I turn to the crowd, against my intuition. "Ok, south side and south side only, would you all like to see Heath Emerald represent you all?"

I lean in to listen to the responses. They sounded very mixed. It seems like the consensus is that he is related to Mr. Emerald, who used to be a civil rights advocate and a staple on the south side, but on the other hand, no one's heard from him in years. Also, I can hear some on the north side murmuring about the mystery involving him and his sister Heather.

"Yeah, she got to be raised on the north and he on the south. Something happened to their lineage. I heard a virus killed almost all of them," a northern Lock said.

"I heard it was a mass suicide," another says.

An aide of Albedo passes the mic to a now standing Mr. Emerald. The look in Heath's eyes was as though he was bracing for him to speak.

* * *

"Hello all, my name is Granger Emerald. I am one of the last surviving members of the Emerald family. Now, this is my distant, yet direct grandson, Heath. It is true that his address is dual, Medley and Blend. Here, he shares the same address as me on the south side district.

"I wanted to preface that, so you all know his status of eligibility as a south side representative. But what I truly want to address is how grateful I am to have two of my descendants vying for the position of Warlock in Medley. It truly breaks my heart to know one of them may have to take that dream from the other, however. One might kill the other. This is coming from a family that was once a great staple in this community, until a ravaging sickness killed off the lot of us.

"Now, only a few Emeralds remain. I cannot force you to choose a different path, Heath, but if you do choose to be a representative for Medley's south side, can you promise to give me a call sometimes? I still raised you, my dear descendant."

The heartfelt words from Mr. Emerald, almost brought me to tears. He genuinely cares about this guy. But what I see in Heath's eyes tells a different story. He seemed unbothered and at certain times, during Mr. Emerald's speech, aloof.

He extends his neck to the podium to address his ancestor's question. "SURE." He says that with little to nothing emoted, however, Mr. Emerald's expression interpreted it differently.

"Then Heath, you have my backing," Mr. Emerald says. He sat back down next to Celeste and the other council members. Heath turns back to me.

"I am ok with you representing the southern district." I hope he doesn't make me regret my decision.

Heath turns to Albedo and places his hand on the green colored combination book. "Heath Emerald, of the Emerald family in Medley. You are sixteen years of age and possess six green HUEs. You are eligible to represent the south side district in the UTT. Do you accept all the rules that come along with the UTT and becoming a Warlock?" Albedo asks.

"I do," Heath says.

"Then I grant you the position. Give it up for Heath."

Many in the crowd expound on claps and cheers, while others saw a different reaction.

Some were unappeased by it.

Some saw it as unappealing.

I shared concern, especially after hearing Mr. Emerald's speech.

I did, however, think this is crunch time and no one else is stepping up. Heath walks over to his circle and passes Ashley, who reaches out to shake his hand. He takes a quick look at her and keeps walking.

She draws her hand back, looking insulted. Phoebe turns to him with a smile, hoping to encourage him to smile back. He never looked down at her, though. He instead kept his eyes on his sister on the other side. They glare back and forth at one another.

I look and see that there were three spots left: "brown," "gold" and "blue." I turn my attention back to the audience.

* * *

"There are three sections left to fill: BROWN, GOLD and BLUE. Will ANY of you, with courage, please step up to fill these spots? Any of you?"

I zero-in on Eve.

I know she sees me staring. But she lowers her head in shame, it seemed. My eyes start shaking. Please Eve, I need you. There is no way she'd blow this opportunity off. Was it all for show?

My eyes almost fall out of my head.

"I will stand with you, Ashe," says Jasper, as he stands in his chair to be seen.

He jumps off the chair and walks up toward the stage. The entire south side erupted in applause, except Celeste and Eve. "Jasper, what the hell are you doing?! You get back here immediately!" Celeste tries to command.

Jasper had already made it to the stage by the time her yells had echoed to the front where he and I stood, however. Eve was in shock too, but she remained motionless to stop him and silent as he reached the top of the steps. Jasper stood in front of me, and his serious expression turned into a smile.

"Ashe, you have become like a brother to me. I can't let you face this challenge alone. Without me, you'd probably get killed," he says. We both laugh. I place my hand on his auburn hair.

"Thank you, buddy!"

He turns around to Albedo. Albedo directs him to place his hand on the brown combination book. He follows suit in the precise spot he was told to place it.

* * *

"Jasper Bistre, of the Bistre family. You are thirteen years of age and have two brown HUEs with one black HUE. You are eligible to take on the Brown Lock's position of Warlock. Do you accept the rules that come along with being a Warlock and swear to abide by the requirements of a Warlock?"

Jasper, without hesitation, says, "I swear."

"Ok Jasper, I grant you permission to represent the south side," Albedo says. The south side goes wild. The claps are outstanding. Jasper takes his spot in the "brown" circle. He shakes Ashley's hand formally and extends his hand to Heath's as well.

Heath does not immediately shake it. Jasper thought it was weird, but Heath briefly shook his hand and turned back toward the crowd.

"Congrats Jasper!" Phoebe says.

"Thank you, Phoebe," he says with a cute little blush.

Amid the clapping, I feel like all sound ceases and all I hear is the sound of Eve breathing all the way in the back. I wonder if she is experiencing this too.

"Eve . . . please," I say under my breath.

Her expression changes as though she heard my request. She stands up and walks toward the stage. I could tell the crowd was not ready to see her walk toward me. The crowd slowly grew quiet the closer and closer she got. My heart felt weak. I am happy she is coming, but the mere sight of her beauty could have made the Roman Empire fall.

She steps up the stairs, and I grab her hand to help her up that final step. "Eve, not you too?" Madam Celeste asks with tears in her eye. I found it sad to see her cry, but humorous watching her blow her nose, all animated and dramatic. Eve and I just stare into each other's eyes. I was still smiling from her standing up.

"Well Ashe, aren't you going to ask me?" she asks jokingly.

"Eve, will you stand next to me and represent the south side?"

Awaiting her response felt like forever.

"Yes, I will stand with you today and every day, until this competition is over," she says, following with an embrace.

The crowd goes wild and jovially makes a resounding "AWE" noise.

We didn't see Matte, but he was noticeably ticked off behind us.

She turns to Albedo, who held the gold book. She places her hand on it.

"Eve, will you accept this position to represent the south side in the UTT?" he asks.

Eve proudly says, "YES."

"Eve, you are sixteen years of age and you are from the noble Gold family in Medley. Nobles have seven HUEs and you have seven gold HUEs. You must be certain that you will represent the south side. Once you swear, there is no coming back," he urges.

It's odd the different way Albedo explained it to her versus everyone on my team. Eve looked at her father, whose eyes shake with anticipation.

* * *

Eve turns back to Albedo. "I swear on my life to abide, Grandlock Albedo."

Albedo pauses for a second before responding, "I grant you permission."

The crowd ignites with applause on the south district, while the north sat in awe. So many on the north district shook their heads, and some even sought to comfort her tearful father.

I couldn't be happier, however. Eve goes and stands in between a happy Jasper and a stoic Heath. Heath, oddly, reaches out to shake her hand, and she accepts.

"Ashe, you have room for one more Lock to complete the south side district. You all need one Lock to vie for the Blue Warlock spot." Albedo says. I turn to the crowd and look around.

No one stood up and no one even moved an inch forward in their seat. This all seems hopeless, but I know I can't give up now when we have come so far.

I look into the crowd, and my eyes catch one familiar face. I blinked repeatedly to make for certain I was not seeing things. YEP! It was definitely him.

"FINNEGAN!" I exclaimed through the mic.

Finnegan, who is making out with one girl from the club the other night, was sitting in the farthest edge of the southern district. He was almost in the west and east section. He stops mid kiss and turns to me on stage.

"Wait, you calling on me, Ashy? Oh shit! Here I come, buddy!" he says.

He almost throws the young lady and runs to the stage. He forgoes walking up the stage and simply jumps up to where I was standing.

Face to face, he reaches to shake my hand. I avoid it, but he then grabs my hand to force a shake.

"OH, don't be like that, Ashy."

I can't keep my rage inside. "YOU JERK! You stole my watch!"

He pauses to think. His face lights up as though a lightbulb turned on. "Oh, this thing? Here you go, brother. Sorry about that!" Finnegan hands over my mother's watch.

I check it for harm, and it was indeed still in mint condition.

I still think this guy is a nut job, but we need a Blue Lock. Plus, he does have blue triangles all over his keychain.

People in the crowd (from every district at that) seemed to not enjoy this pick, but not for the reasons as before.

"Hey, I think that asshole stole my house ornaments," says one person.

"I remember letting him spend the night with me and I caught him walking out with my jewelry. When I tried to confront him, he made a puddle that I kept slipping on," says a young lady.

Finnegan turns his amiable energy to Albedo, who laughs under his breath, but then puts on a serious tone. "Finnegan Blue, you are of the Blue family lineage here in Medley and you are seventeen years of age. You have seven blue HUEs, which makes you a descendent of a noble family. Your ancestor, my colleague, wanted me to spare you from jail since you were the last of her lineage in Medley. BUT, she left her position and has since left town. You're the only remaining member of the Blue family in Medley now. Do you wish to join the UTT and solemnly swear to abide by all rules and requirements?"

"Absolutely, I'm down to represent the south side!" he responds.

The south side claps loudly once more.

Finnegan heads to his section, but not before Albedo grabs him by the shoulder and gestures to Finnegan to return the blue combination book. Albedo sternly warned Finnegan, "Your larcenous behavior will no longer be tolerated. Your ancestor is no longer here. You will no longer be spared."

Finnegan smiles brightly and returns the book back to Albedo. He stands next to Heath on one side and Phoebe on the other. Heath looked confused and leans in on Finnegan. "Wouldn't you already have a Blue family combination book? What would be the purpose of stealing that one?"

"Dude, that one belongs to my ancestor. I wanted to just hold it a little longer, is all," he responds. Heath looked even more confused, but simply turns back around to face the crowd.

"Well south district, these are your representatives!" Albedo says and all give a standing ovation, including him. He directs me to go stand next to Phoebe, on the end.

I follow suit and I catch a glimpse of everyone on the other team looking in an array of unique expressions when seeing me. Albedo turns to the middle section.

"Now it is time for the west district, then finally the east."

* * *

A woman with large glasses waste no time standing up with a short note. "Due to the highly sensitive matter that came about in choosing Alabaster Black to be in the UTT, the west district, along with the east district, have both opted out of participating in this year's UTT. We do not wish to risk any harm of involvement that could occur and the potential bloodshed that comes along with a possessor of an active Black Key. With that, the west and east fully endorse the north district. We look forward to seeing you all persevere in this uphill battle."

She sits down as quick as she stood up.

I was completely caught off guard, and I tried to hide my expression. All six Locks I chose, stare down at me to gauge my face.

Albedo turns to the west district council, and no one challenges this woman's assessment. Thus, Albedo moves on, "Ok, then that is that. This UTT will be solely north versus south. You fourteen are to return home and await further instruction from my aides. Anyone who harms, steals from, or inconveniences any of these potential Warlocks will face prosecution. As of today, you all are officially representatives of your two respective districts and should act accordingly. Any questions?"

None of the northern district nor any of mine had any response to Albedo.

A small, telling smirk comes across his face. "The UTT is now in assembly."

Kiss and Tell

The night grew calm after the town's council meeting. Back in the house, Jasper, Eve, Finnegan, and I were all facing a verbal lashing from Celeste. After she hit me across the head twice with a rolled piece of paper for allowing Jasper to join the UTT, she made dinner to which we all enjoyed.

She spoke pleasantly while we were eating.

"CONGRATULATIONS—my soon to be Warlocks."

We didn't have it in us to address the complete switch to her personality. But we all took it for what it was, and in unity said, "Thank you, Madam Celeste." After dinner, I helped Eve do the dishes, while Jasper showed Finnegan where he would be sleeping since he wanted to spend the night with us.

When walking Finnegan through the hallway, Jasper noticed that every time he turned around to Finnegan, there were objects missing off the walls. He made sure to shake him down in the bedroom. "Empty your pockets!"

A few hours pass and Celeste had fallen asleep on the couch. Her snores drown out the cyclic news playing. On the screen, a balanced looking woman talks about the UTT council meeting that was held earlier. All seven of us had to pose for the news after the council, and that picture was displayed on screen. "These are the seven Locksmiths that have been chosen to represent the southern district of Medley. The southern district historically has never had a real voice in political matters, but now, with the introduction of these new hopefuls, the southern district is seeking retribution from what many have stated are centuries worth of injustices," she says.

In our picture, you see me in the center with Finnegan's arm around me in a playful chokehold and smiling. Eve was on the other side of me with her arm wrapped around mine and her other arm pulling Ashley closer in on the picture. Ashley looked a bit uncomfortable in her embrace, and her smile exemplified it. Jasper and Phoebe were the shortest, so they stood in front in an embrace, smiling. Heath stood off on the side with his arms folded. This was a tight picture, so he was close, but his back was turned to us.

The news lady had the mic in front of a very pale man with black eyes, holding his daughter, who shared the same physical features. "Sir, what do you think about this all?" she asks him.

"I think it's great that my district will finally be heard," he tearfully said. "We Black Locks need more unity," he finishes.

The scene shifts to an unsettling portrait of a man's court appearance. The news lady continues, "Now, in breaking news, Kindle Mars has a trial set for the 22nd day in the Red month. Kindle's bail is 1,000 tokens, and he maintains his innocence."

Kindle, behind bars, comes across the camera to speak to the news. "I know true justice will prevail and I know through the HUE, all is possible in the universe. So, I am awaiting the day Albedo gives me a call to say I'm free from all of this. There have been exceptions in the past to this 'no quaternary' rule for other Locks, so I just don't see a difference between them and myself.

Is it my eye color?"

Outside, we all sit around the bonfire pit in the backyard.

It was cold outside, but the blistering flame made it cozy.

Around the pit were four logs laid in a diamond shape. We each sat on a log: Eve, Finnegan, Jasper and myself. We all sat in a peaceful silence, with everyone looking lost in thought. The enormity of our selection sank in. The plaid shirt I was wearing was borrowed from Finnegan, but of course, there is no telling where he got it from. We all sit among each other and vibe, with the night sky showing the most beautiful stars I could imagine.

"Well, everyone, looks like we are Medley's finest." My attempt to break the ice felt unaccomplished.

Everyone seemed a bit tensed up.

Finnegan was more relaxed. "So wait, the district makes the laws and we just enforce them? Sounds like easy work to me."

Jasper nods. "Yes, we get to determine whether to certify or decline each law. However, that's assuming we win. There is no guarantee that we will certify anything," he says. Jasper looks more solemn and concerned.

"Don't worry little guy, we got this!" I tried to cheer him up, but his face was stuck on worry. Truth is, I was just as uncertain about the ins and outs of this tournament as the next person.

Eve looks more disconcerting as she stared off in her own direction, aloof from our conversation. "I would have never wished to take this spot from another girl," Eve says noiselessly.

* * *

I sympathized, but I would be lying if I said I wasn't happy it was her over somebody else.

"I am excited! How often does someone get the opportunity to run the town?" Finnegan speaks with eager.

"This is a role that comes with great responsibility," Jasper says as he lays his chin on his clasps hands.

"You are not starting to second guess, are you kiddo?" Finnegan asks to which he swiftly denies.

"I am just thinking about everything. I will commit to anything I sign myself up for, but this tournament decreases our life expectancy. I guess I am having a hard time dealing with the rationale of that."

"There is a possibility of death every time you step outside, Jappers. You gotta take life by the sword and continue to fight the perilous war it wages on you," Finnegan says.

"Yeah, except I don't usually go looking for it. We all just signed up to compete against a group of Locks who've been socialized to hate and destroy us. They view the best of us as scum," Jasper says.

"Jasper, don't speak so pessimistically. You have the three of us to protect you. With Ashe on our team, we can rest assured that his Key is a safety net," Eve says in a tranquil way. Jasper visibly looks calmer.

"Yeah little bud, as long as I'm around, I'll make it my prerogative that we all make it back safe." I scoot over to his log and give him a slight hug.

* * *

"We got this." I position my wrist next to his. Both of our keychains touch and Jasper looks at our comparative colored triangles. I had one, and he had about twenty. "We are going to grow. Soon all of those triangles will be brown and all mine black, little buddy."

Jasper seemed receptive to that and smiles in recognition. I look at Eve and we make eye contact. No words were stated, but I felt that she affirmed what I said to Jasper. Finnegan takes notice to our gaze at one another.

"Hey Jasper, why don't I take you inside, bro? You look a little sleepy and we got a big week ahead of us."

Jasper yawns and stays stagnant at first, but then stands up. "Yeah, it's past my bedtime," he says. He and Finnegan walk toward the backdoor.

Finnegan pats his back as they walk in and inconspicuously turns around to wink with his thumb up to me.

I look up at Eve. Her beautiful face looked even more attractive from the glow of the fire. We made eye contact and awkwardly giggle.

Our small laughter ceases, and I rise nervously to sit beside her on her log. To my surprise, she wasn't shy or uneasy about it (unlike me, of course). Now, looking her in her stunning pair of gold eyes, I ask, "How are you doing?"

Taking a moment to think, she answered, "I believe that it is called cognitive dissonance. It's when you have two conflicting views.

"On the one hand, I want Black Locks to be liberated from oppression, but I just don't want to take the opportunity from a Black Lock. I also know I have a privileged position that allows me to speak for those who don't have a voice in society. So, it's just a lot." She said it all with an unwavering smile.

* * *

"I could see how that could be stressful."

We make brief eye contact and I set it in my head that this was the moment.

This is the one swing at the bat I can make and maybe she'll allow it. I lean in and slowly raise my lips to hers. She did not resist and, in fact, she grabs my face as if to pull closer to hers. This is it, I begin to think. Just one inch away and she backs out. She turns her head and blushes in embarrassment.

"I'm sorry Ashe. This is my fault."

"Eve, no it's my bad. I don't want to move too quick or anything. This is all new to me, too." Eve switches from embarrassed to an amused tone.

"Wait Ashe, have you never kissed a girl?"

I shy away from answering and turn my head. "Oh, that is so cute. I didn't know that." She pinches my cheeks in a daunting way. To pretend I didn't like it, I kept a serious face, although I did. "I apologize Ashe," she says, and she lets my cheek go. My smile lets her know I'm not upset.

"Have you ever kissed a guy?" I wait to gauge her reaction.

She hesitates, but takes a deep sigh. "Yes, but that's a long story."

I look alert. "Tell me, I'm listening."

She holds herself in a scared, protective position. Lowering her head, I could tell something painful was on her mind. I consoled her with a hand on her shoulder. She takes a deep breath before channelling gold HUE. "I would like you to get a good visual while I speak. Unlock."

* * *

The gold HUE covers the small area and before me is the moving picture of a youthful Eve. She walks downstairs to greet her father's guest.

"I was so excited to meet this young boy who he had talked about so much. He seemed like a nice guy at first."

Eve changes the image to her and a curly haired male playing outside in the backyard.

My eyes widen. "Is that Matte?!"

She nods yes. Suspiciously, they both have grey eyes.

"Wait, why are your eyes grey?"

"Oh no, no one told you. So, when we are kids, all Locks have grey eyes. Our eyes don't change colors until our Keys reveal themselves. The exception being Black Locksmiths like yourself. Sorry, we forgot to tell you!" She smiles and of course I forgave her.

Come to think, I don't believe I have seen any kids other than Black ones since I have been here.

Eve draws attention back to the light show and continues, "Something about him felt safe. I think it was my trust in my father that fostered that relationship. He was friendly and outgoing. He was so sweet when we were younger."

The scene changes to her spacious field of a backyard. Her father informs her that Matte had arrived.

"Ok daddy, well I am going to go hide from him," Eve says. Her father laughs, while she quickly runs to find a decent sized tree to stand behind.

She awaits in the silent air. Only her breathing is audible before she covers her mouth.

"BOO!" Matte says. Eve jumps in terror.

"You scared me! If it were nighttime, I'd think you were a Deadlock," she said, laughing. "How did you find me?"

"Guess," he says with a smile. She looked closer and notices his eyes were gold now.

"OH my HUE, Matte! Your Key revealed itself! That is so exciting!" She gives him a friendly embrace, then she pulls back and smiles at him innocently.

"Now, I have this weird ability to read electrical impulses in the brain. I could hear you thinking a yard away."

Present day Eve narrates, "He then promised me that he would never read my mind without my permission. He would sometimes use it to figure out which cabinet my dad hid the snacks. He was the nicest guy in the world. But all of that came crashing down when he did what he did," she says.

"What did he do?" I honestly wasn't sure I was ready for an answer.

Eve replaces the image with one of herself and friends in a treehouse. Now her eye color is gold, and she looked about thirteen. A younger Eve blushes at the sight of another boy with darker features and eyes similar to hers.

"We would play 'house' or 'clubhouse,' he called it, and he was the only boy who could kiss me." The image shows Matte leaning in to kiss Eve. She looked uncomfortable, but accepts the kiss. A subtle spark of electricity can be seen once their lips locked. He leans away and Eve looked embarrassed.

"I would always feel embarrassed, especially around the guy I actually liked. But little did I know, he was my first kiss . . . and . . . my last."

I look to present day Eve and tears form in her eyes. It was just a kiss, from my perspective. However, my intuition was telling me there was more to the story.

"What, did his breath stink?" I tried to joke, but it fell flat. Eve shows another image of her with the young male she actually liked and he attempted to give her a kiss. He leaned in on her innocent face and puckers his lips. The moment they kissed, electricity from her lips slices his mouth open and draws blood. The boy looks wildly dismayed and jets from the scene.

A young teen, Eve, stands there looking perplexed and confused.

"That was shocking, Eve, no pun intended."

"Ashe, to sum it all up, he used a combination that made it so that anyone that tries to kiss me will be repelled by electricity."

I gasped. "Wow," is the only thing I can say. I give her an embrace and the light show ends.

"Ashe, this would happen every time I kissed a boy other than him in the treehouse. I finally came to my senses and couldn't take it anymore. I told my father and he told me that I should be more loyal to Matte." Eve wipes her tears and sighs.

* * *

"Truth is, Ashe, my father arranged for Matte to be my husband when I was young. He and Matte's dad came to an agreement on behalf of their children. His son would be able to elevate into noble status, and his daughter would marry a rich solid with status."

I am lost for words. Her dad sounds manipulative. I wonder if he told Matte to do that to Eve. If so, he's not only deceptive, but a monster.

"What does he get out of pawning you off to some dude? Can't you choose to marry a rich guy you ACTUALLY like?"

She tearfully responds, "It's about the purity of our lineage. As long as I marry and have kids with someone with all gold HUEs, all of our children will be Goldsmiths and my lineage will dominate, because I have seven gold HUEs. My father is just retaining power."

"Well, if it matters, I would be jealous to see you kiss another guy too."

In my head, that sounded more romantic than it sounded coming out of my mouth.

Her expression told a different story. "Ashe, I have had to deal with this my whole life. The only person that can reverse this is him. My father could've press charges but refused! That is one of the reasons I left. I don't want to be a part of that elitist cesspool. That combination should be illegal!" she cries.

Poor girl. Seeing her like this makes me want to take justice into my own hands.

Wait, I CAN.

"I have a solution, Eve. Let's make each other a promise. When we become

Warlocks, we can pressure the council to create a law that would ban that combo. We will make sure no girl experiences this again." Eve smiles, signifying she felt a little more at ease I think.

"And as far as Matte goes. I promise to force him to reverse that combo before the UTT is done. How does that sound?"

She looks at me, inspired. "You'd do that for me, Ashe?"

"OF COURSE! I have an active Black Key," I joke.

She leans in and touches my nose with hers. "Ashe, if you can do that for me, I'd be honored to give you your first kiss."

My body trembles at the sound of her voice. I shake and almost collapse, but I hold it together. She immediately puts her hands on my face and flirtatiously pushes my head backward.

"SIKE." She laughs at me and turns toward the backdoor.

The fire starts to go out, as she walks back toward the house. I can't tell if she is mocking me. Did she mean what she said or not?

She blows a subtle kiss at me before walking into the house.

"Good-night Ashe," she says while still laughing.

"Be careful. I don't want to get electrocuted," I retort.

Smooth Ashe, smooth.

House Rules

Red 8th, a Wednesday, and here I am surrounded by darkness, once more. I feel myself diving deep into the abyss and before I know it, I am standing in front of that black door again.

Chained and locked, I reach out to touch the padlock, but stop midrange. I just stand at the door.

"Ashe, you've come to visit me two nights in a row and haven't said a word. Is there something you want?" Enyracl asks.

"No, or at least I am not sure as of now. I am not certain how to feel about you."

"Well, you'll never find certainty without conversing with me, right?"

I halt before responding. "I don't know if I should trust you. Last time I did, you murdered Medley's leadership. You're the sole reason for all this disarray."

Silence fell on us both.

* * *

I awaited his response.

"So, what is it that warrants this visit, Ashe?"

I pause and now I'm unable to respond.

"You know something about my past. You know my parents. You know where I come from. I want to know. Tell me Enyracl!"

My body starts to tremble. But he responds with more silence on the other side of the door.

"In due time, Ashe," he says. I feel myself instantly being pushed out of my 'inner core.' That's what I call this miasma of darkness that surpasses even my padlock in depth.

I travel further and further through the darkness until I'm pushed outside myself, back into my regular consciousness.

"Are you ok, Ashe?" Jasper asks. I open my eyes. I was sitting on the steps of Celeste's front porch, watching the rainfall. The awning prevented the heavy rain from touching me.

Next to me were Eve and Jasper, along with our three black duffle bags.

"You fell asleep again, Ashe." Eve says in a concerned voice.

"He still hasn't gotten any good sleep. All through the night, he's been waking up," Jasper notes.

"I am just dealing with my inner demon." I stand out and stretch.

* * *

I guess I could also say that I was a bit stressed about this impending court visit that was supposed to be scheduled for today.

No one has mentioned it since I was chosen to be in the UTT, so I certainly wasn't going to bring it up.

Eve approaches and places her hand on my shoulder.

"Is Enyracl still daunting you to release him from behind the door?" she asks.

"Well, to be honest, I've been curiously seeking him. I know he knows more about my past than I do, but I don't know whether to trust him.

"So, I'm a little conflicted."

Eve and Jasper both pat me on the back to comfort. We were all waiting on the carriage ride to take us to Albedo's castle.

His instructions in letters sent to us all individually were to pack dress clothing and downtime clothing. Apparently, the everything else would be supplied.

Or almost everything. Special instructions included packing: toothpaste, brush/comb, make-up, bras (for ladies), glasses as required (no colored contacts), watches are permissible (thank God!), soap and hygiene materials, combination books, any material that is relevant to your use of combinations (staffs, swords, tactical weapons, etc.), only one weapon per person and lastly, our orders that state we are officially participating in the UTT.

The latter, I held in my hand in a black envelope. My watch is in my pocket in the box it came in and I stood awaiting patiently on the carriage to arrive.

* * *

We had already told Madam Celeste our goodbyes and now we await the ride.

One thing extra I carried with me was a bible.

I found it in Celeste's miscellaneous box in the attic, labeled "spirituality from the past." I took it and have been reading it throughout the night when I can't sleep.

The sound of a vehicle from the sky takes my attention. A decent sized carriage with a zebra balloon lands in the yard. Through the windows, I can see a cheery, young fellow driving it. His clothing resembled Albedo's guards' uniforms, so I assumed he was one.

"All aboard!" he calls. The three of us grab our duffle bags and head into the carriage. "Hello, my Warlocks to be! Top of the morning to you," he greets us.

We all get in and buckle up in the back. "Hello to you, sir. With time, you will see us stepping into that light as Warlocks," Eve cheerfully says.

"Oh, I don't doubt it." With a flip of the lasso, the balloon rises and so does the carriage.

We fly high above the rainy sky and soar gently over the horizon of Medley. The more we approach the castle in the vista, the more it really sets in that this is real.

A little less than half an hour later and I see the castle. The rain made it look more mysterious than my prior visit. "Does this count as the first day?" Jasper asks.

"I mean, you can look at it that way if you'd like. But the purpose of today is acquainting you all with the tournament's structure. Day 1 or day 0 are acceptable ascriptions," the guard says.

We narrowly shoot through the wind to land the carriage. Landing in the courtyard, there's a massive mix of hellish wind and pounding rainfall.

The wind blew hard enough for Eve to have to open the door twice to get out of the carriage. We rush in the rain to get all our stuff. The guard jumps out with an umbrella, directing us toward the entrance to the castle. "Let's go, let's go," he says, waving his hand in the direction of the entrance.

We get through the entryway and don't make it three steps before the guard directs us to put our duffle bags in a row entitled "South." We place all our bags in a row and there were already three bags placed. The names on the bags were ARIES, EMERALD & SATURN, in all caps. I walk over and drop my bag at the end in the "black" square, and I'm met by a female guard with my name tag. "Here you are, sir. Just place this right here," she says, clipping my tag on my bag.

She follows suit to do the same with Eve and Jasper. I notice Finnegan's last name is missing.

The guard directs us to a room where the other representatives stood. In the first row, the north section stood with all of their UTT representatives in assembly.

Standing in order from front to back: Fenix, Amber, Matte, Heather, Ark, Jay & Roan. They stood facing forward with their arms down by their waist. They seemed the least perturb by the three of us arriving. Forward, they faced two huge closed curtains, one black and one white.

Parallel to them, on the other side of the room, was the south section: Ashley, Heath and Phoebe. They didn't stand in line like the other group.

* * *

Ashley looked annoyed by Phoebe talking about her balloons. "I have a red horse named 'Rusty,' a blue and white horse named 'Merle' and I have a yellow horse—" she continued.

Adjacent to them, laying on the wall with his arms folded, was Heath. He had a piece of wheat hanging from his mouth like a farmer, and he seemed aloof from the other two.

There was no sign of Finnegan.

We walk over to the trio and greet them. "Hello everyone, how's it going?" Eve asks with a bright smile and eager tone.

Phoebe gives her a hug, but fails to hug Jasper, whose arms open for embrace. Instead, she ran past him and jumped to hug my waist.

"Savior, I knew you would show up." I give her an awkward hug before peeling her off my lower half. She eventually sees Jasper and gives him a hug.

He visibly seemed enamored by it. His face blushing so red I almost couldn't tell his hair from his skin.

"Hello, Ashley Aries. How are you doing?" Eve greets.

Something about her expression seems unimpressed by Eve.

"You should just call me Ashley and I am doing well," she responds in a stern way. Eve laughs it off and tries to hug Ashley. Ashley cuts her off, pointing her finger at the clock. The clock says 12:58 pm.

"You were almost late. The message said to be here at 1:00 pm. Do you have the message that Albedo sent?"

Eve's voice shrinks a bit. "I do."

Sternly, Ashley responds, "Then you will do well being more punctual. I got here before every Lock in this room." Eve is taken aback, but chooses to continue to smile and project positivity.

"Oh, I love how punctual you are. And they try to say Black Locks are always late. Girl, you are proving them wrong every step of the way, and I love that for you." Eve says, placing her hand on Ashley's shoulder.

Ashley didn't acknowledge it, but utters a simple question, "Them?"

I walk over to the wall and Heath only turns to look my way when I am a foot away from him. "You need something?" Heath asked pointedly.

"I just wanted to say hello and speak." Heath turns his head to me.

"Ok?" he inquires.

"Has anyone seen Finnegan?" I asked.

"I have been here the longest and I can confirm he has not come in here once." Ashley says.

I wonder if he's alright or whether he got cold feet at the end.

"Phoebe, who's taking over the paper route since you're here?" Jasper asks her.

"My cousin said she could do it while I am here," she responds, cutely.

* * *

"We should probably lineup, it's nearing the start time," Ashley says.

Heath grunts. "Why? What's the point of lining up without instructions to do so?"

Ashely gets annoyed. "Well, the circles on the ground imply that's where we should stand, just like the other group. There are circles on the ground in the same order as the north district."

"We don't even have everyone here, so we are already out of order with these made up rules you're talking about," he retorts.

Ashley visibly looks infuriated.

I turned to the side after the whole debacle, and notice the entire north district's Warlock wannabes were staring at us intensely.

"Hey you two, how about we go stand in the circles and see what happens? Plus, we don't want to look disunited next to our adversaries," Eve says very soft-spoken, but with a sense of urgency.

Heath twists the wheat in his mouth with his tongue as if to show disinterest, but he eventually is the first to go to his respective circle. Followed by Jasper, then me, and Phoebe—who literally was following me.

I position her in her circle, but she couldn't help but stare up at me. I politely turn her around and she remains.

"See girly, problem solved," Eve cheerfully says to Ashley. She, however, does not share the same cheer. Eve walks to her respective spot and we wait.

* * *

Not two minutes pass and the curtains start to open. It was a giant television screen that covered both sides of the wall from corner to corner.

A male guard comes in front of us all and stands with his hands positioned at the sides of his hips. "We will now conduct the UTT purpose," he says. He then pauses for a moment of silence. Facing us, he looks forward in the middle of the two districts.

I even turn around inconspicuously to make sure no one was behind us. He does a left-face and walks off to the side.

The television comes on and it's a scene with Albedo sitting at his desk and staring through the screen. He looked mighty fresh and professional in his all black robe. He dawned a rather serious expression. A voice from behind becomes audible. "Wait Ashy, don't start without me!"

I turn around and it is none other than Finnegan. He runs and grabs a hold of my shoulder for a quick squeeze. "Sorry about being late. The girl I was staying with put me out. So I had to go stay with another girl I was talking to and then she found out about the other girl I was talking to. Long story short, Ashy, Albedo's aides found it hard to find me. BUT NOW I'M HERE."

I simply reply, "Good."

Finnegan goes and stands in between Phoebe and Heath. "So, this blue circle is for me?"

The other group has several members laughing at Finnegan. That is until a stringent Fenix turns around and silences them. He got his whole row in order, then only turned back toward the television when there was not a decibel of sound left behind him.

* * *

Albedo, on the screen, begins, "At this point, you all should be in the room. There is always a straggler, but after today there will be no more.

"Welcome to the UTT, also known as the Unlocking the Truth Tournament. All of you were hand selected under the guidelines of the World Constitution and the Medley Articles that contextualize them. Each of you represents a different Key combination, making no two people in this room completely identical, not even the twins Heath and Heather." After he says that last part, Heath and Heather glare at one another. Heather dawns that creepy smile, while Heath turns back to the screen.

Albedo continued, "Similar to a specialized training facility, you should treat the UTT as such. This is a House to give you guidelines to becoming a successful Warlock and one day, one of you, will take over my role as Grandlock.

"But that is further down the line. In this competition, you will showcase your skills against the offending team, and the winners will face legislation from your district. This competition displays Medley the fair option of allowing different Locks the opportunity to assume the Grandlock position and potentially change the governing scheme here in Medley. As you all know, Medley is the beacon of the world.

"Whatever rules we accept, so must the other towns in Aether.

"Whatever governing we have, they must adopt it as well. Currently, we are being watched by the world as Warlocks in every town in Aether are sending me messages daily.

"The consensus is, if I am omniscient, then I must know how the UTT will end. I tell the leaders as I tell you all: THE FUTURE CAN CHANGE. Thus, in an effort to maintain balance, I will allow this to play itself out. Revelations about the future can massively disrupt predetermined events."

The scene with Albedo ends. The guard comes back to the center of the room.

"The UTT gameplay," he announces, looking straight forward, sternly.

He then moves to the side of the room.

The screen switches to an overhead of the Arcane Forest. It looked like whatever had filmed this had hovered above it.

Albedo still narrates,

"The UTT is a House, but also a competitive trial. Locksmiths from each district will compete weekly to defeat one another in rounds of tests. In these rounds, each district will employ combat, logic and HUE against opposing teams. If any member chooses to go rogue against their team, they will be banished from the UTT and ultimately dealt with in court. As UTT members, you all are bound by oath that you will now work together as a team and conquer as a team. If you lose, you lose as a team.

"We will conduct a new round, every Wednesday. We will crown the sole winner of each round, 'Warlock of the week.' Then, the legislative branch of the winner's respective district will put forth a law to be examined. The presenting Warlock of the winning team will announce whether they will go ahead with or disregard each legislation. Even if someone is crowned Warlock of the week, they may pass the announcement and power to make said determination to another Lock of their district. If a presenting Lock may die before the announcement, the Locksmiths of the council will vote on who they wish to examine and make a determination on the law.

"Every month in 4003 will have 7-8 weeks. This means we'll have seven rounds each month, using the extra week for rest."

The screen shifts to what looks like a giant crayon. It was as wide as Jasper from shoulder to shoulder, and I would say about 5 feet 6 inches tall. The tip pointed into the air like an arrow, giving it that distinct crayon look. On the side is a scale that started at the bottom and goes to the middle of this object.

"This is a tower. These objects have an inner frame, completely made from meteor remnants. The exterior is coated with a special material, making them susceptible to specific HUE on the checks and balances scale. This particular tower is red, meaning it is more susceptible to blue HUE and so forth, etc.

"Weekly, Locksmiths will try to inflict as much damage to this tower to top the scale and end the round. Each week, the tournament will give each team a tower or towers. When a team conquers the opposing team's tower, the round is over. Locks will hear a blasting noise from my castle saying that this week's round is over.

"Once over, all combat is to cease and there will be no more harm done to either the group or their towers. As the weeks go on, there will be a new set of towers that match the number of weeks. Week four will have four towers and week five will have five, for example.

"Each week will have different colored towers than the previous weeks. Tomorrow is week one, and each district will receive one tower. The system randomizes and identifies the colors the night before each round.

"The Locks of each district will determine who will be staying to protect the towers and who will be going to conquer the opposing district's towers. When conquered, the following day will have legislation from the council of the winning team announced.

* * *

"The winning team will announce the representative that will be making a judgment on this law or these laws. The number of legislative acts that will be reviewed will coincide with the number of weeks and towers. Therefore, on weeks where there are multiple towers, the first team to destroy them all before the other will get to judge the legislation presented by their respective council. In the event that multiple Locks destroy towers on the opposing team, the winning team's district will vote on who will be the Warlock of the week, and ultimately who will decide the determination of the legislation.

"Announcements of laws will occur every Friday of that round's week. This Friday will represent the first law being judged by the winning team's announcer. All Locks will get paid on Friday of every week. The pay will be a base of 1,400 tokens. A Lock cannot be Warlock of the week twice in a row, however, can be bestowed that title more than once in a month. On the final week of each month, the districts will vote on who they would like to see face off in a gladiator style match.

"While killing is permitted, this match can end in a knockout. This individual will be Warlock of the week and will determine the outcomes of seven legislation. The amount of combatants for this final round will increase monthly. Example: the Brown month will have two individuals per district, Gold month three, Green month four, etc.

"The ultimate winner of the UTT will come from the victor or victors of the final week brawl in the last month, the Black month. Respectfully, by this time, the townsfolk of Medley will be acquainted with your system of governance that each of you will individually choose.

"The winning district will choose which representatives' ideals they want to see govern. With that, the very first chance you are given to be Warlock of the Week, you must choose from a list of governing systems that you wish to represent. That system you must maintain throughout the tournament. Once chosen, you are not allowed to choose a different governance.

"There will be token distributions to Locks in Medley, depending on the Warlock that wins governance choice. For example, if one of you wins and chooses the aristocratic governance, there will automatically be 700 additional tokens paid out to all the citizens of Medley that come from noble families. The payouts do not neglect those of an opposing district.

"Lastly, Medley represents the heart of Aether. Laws that are approved here are expected to be implemented everywhere in the world. Thus, Medley is the litmus test. Only the last standing Warlock crowned Grandlock on that final week will determine governance not only here, but all over Aether. The other towns have no immediate impetus to change their laws to match ours, until then. With that, I wish you all a great UTT. This competition begins, NOW."

The screen turns off on Albedo's final speech. A moment of silence allows all the representatives in the room to assess what was said. That was a lot, but the gist of the instructions are that we have a lot weighing on us as representatives. The guard walks back to the center of the room with a list.

"Everyone, listen up! These are the Warlock House rules:

1.) All representatives of the UTT will be expected to participate, after hearing the reading of the rules, until the final week of the Black month or until everyone from the other district is dead.

2.) Representatives will not be allowed to resign from this House.

3.) Wednesdays starting at 7 am, all representatives will be outside their house dressed professionally in their battle gear and standing in front of their respective line.

* * *

4.) Rounds end at the voice of Albedo coming from the castle.

5.) In the event there is no winner beyond 7 pm, there will be a TKO style fight between one Lock chosen from each district as determined by the representatives of each group solely.

6.) Wednesdays are the only days of the week whereby any physical harm may be permitted on the opposing team, including, but not limited to, killing.

7.) Any harm done to your own teammates can result in expulsion from the UTT and legal issues that can place you in prison for the rest of your life. Exceptions are in the case of sparring with teammates that does not result in death and are agreed upon by all parties.

8.) At no point will tertiary or quaternary combinations be used outside of the final week round of each month.

9.) Saturdays and Sundays are personal days in which all remaining representatives will go to their respective homes and will not return any later than 7 am Monday morning. During this time, Albedo's aides will clean the houses you all will occupy during the tournament, change the sheets, and repair any damaged appliances.

10.) Because you are now officially in the UTT, any prior convictions or court orders are automatically removed and expunged from your records."

That last rule almost made me collapse with relief. No longer do I have to go to court for that night out with Finnegan.

The aide continues,

"11.) As representatives, minor rules in the World Constitution no longer apply to you all. That includes, but is not limited to: curfew, petty crimes under 51 tokens, gambling on the street for sums less than 101 tokens, stalking for more than 2 hours, etc. All major crimes are still in effect and will cost you twice the consequence if committed. This includes, but is not limited to: killing another Hueman or regional protective species, stealing with a sum of more than 50 tokens, rape, destruction of property that exceeds more than 1000 tokens, etc.

12.) You all legally will be living amongst one another for a year unless the UTT ends for you in death or the entire opposing team is killed. To promote proper bonding, for the sake of your districts you all represent, you are required to all sit for breakfast at 7 am and dinner at 7 pm. Both must be prepared by you all. Wednesdays, you will not be required to have this bonding time. Out of respect, unless invited, you are to never intrude inside the other district's house without permission.

13.) Weekly, you all will be replenished with food in the fridge, but if it were to run out before the weekend, you all are responsible for forging your own meals and eating among one another still counts.

14.) Lastly, in the event someone dies during a round, their body will be handed over to their families and everyone, including the person who may have resulted in their death, will attend any funeral or remembrance. If no family member claims the individual, they will be subject to cremation and personal ceremony among the remaining representatives."

The guard rolls the list up and places it in his pocket. "You all will be handed individual copies of this list upon exiting the castle. With that, these are the rules and expectations of gameplay for the UTT. You all have been read them and from this point on, you are officially under these guidelines. An aide will show each of you to your respective homes. Are there any disagreements?"

* * *

We all stand quietly in the room, awaiting someone to speak up about a grievance, if any. No one spoke. A tiny hand raises and it belonged to Phoebe.

"Is the home we are staying at going to be in the view of the castle?" she asks.

"Yes," the guard says, confused.

"Good, because the Arcane Forest has many Deadlocks in it. They shelter in the darkness, because they are afraid of the light. I feel safer knowing Granddaddy Lock Albedo will not be far," she says ever so innocently.

The guard laughs. "My dear, Grandlock Albedo will not be saving you from any impending death. If you succumb to a Deadlock, that will be ruled 'death by natural causes.' I'd encourage you all to never go into the forest alone, if you are worried."

Phoebe quivers with fear. I place my hand on her shoulder and assure her. "Don't worry, I got your back."

The guard looks around, and no other questions were held.

With a spine-chilling smirk, the guard says, "Ok, let's take you all to your new homes. As Grandlock Albedo has said, the UTT starts, NOW."

www.ingramcontent.com/pod-product-compliance
Lightning Source LLC
Chambersburg PA
CBHW061444030726
47503CB00005B/1562